Accounting

for

Football

ABSOLUTELY AMAZING eBOOKS

Habent Sua Fata Libelli

ABSOLUTELY AMAZING eBOOKS

Manhanset House
Shelter Island Hts., New York 11965-0342

bricktower@aol.com • tech@absolutelyamazingebooks.com
• absolutelyamazingebooks.com

The Absolutely Amazing eBooks colophon is a trademark of J. T. Colby & Company, Inc.

Library of Congress Cataloging-in-Publication Data
McMillan, Steve
Accounting For Football.
p. cm.
        1. FICTION / Mystery & Detective / Amateur Sleuth.
        2. FICTION / Mystery & Detective / General.
        3. FICTION / Thrillers / Suspense.
        Fiction, I. Title.
        ISBN: 978-1-955036-59-7 Trade Paper
        ISBN: 978-1-955036-60-3 Hardcover

October 2023

Accounting

for

Football

Steve McMillan

Accounting Mysteries

By Steve McMillan

Accounting Can Be Murder
Accounting And Murder Around The World
Accounting For Vampires
Accounting For Pirates
Accounting Isn't Always Kosher

Available from
AbsolutelyAmazingEbooks.com

Table of Contents

Acknowledgments

Thanks to Fran, Norah, Regina, and Margaret.
Thanks to Shirrel and John.
Thanks to Emily, Mikayla, Mike, Matt, and Liam.
And, as always, thanks to Debbi for being Debbi.
THANKS A LOT, KK!

Chapter One

Len Meadows was a backup linebacker for the New York Giants. He wasn't a starter but got a fair amount of playing time. He was hoping he got to play today at just the right moment.

The Philadelphia Eagles were playing the Giants at the Eagles home field, Lincoln Financial Field. It was December, and both teams were sitting on 8-4 records. They had equally been having solid seasons and were tied in the standings of the NFC East. Every game they had left was important, particularly since they had another game against each other at MetLife Stadium in early January.

The Eagles had spent much of the season focusing on their running game, which was unusual considering the NFL offensive plans of most teams. All the teams had some running attacks, but almost all paid most of their attention to the passing game. The Eagles' top running back, Franklin Johns, was having a breakout year. He was already over a thousand yards, 1,180, with 12 touchdowns. He wouldn't set any NFL records, but he was clearly leading the team to a solid season. His backup, Billy Sans, was also having a solid year, and when Johns needed a break, Sans usually did an admirable job of stepping up.

The Eagles and Giants were in the third quarter, with the Eagles were up 20-13 and the ball on the 50-yard line. It was third and five. The Giants decided to play it safe and sent only three defensive linemen into the game. Len Meadows was brought in as another linebacker.

Most teams in today's NFL would call a passing play on a third and five call, but the Eagles sent Johns right up the middle. He got past the defensive linemen and made it into the secondary. One of the linebackers grabbed Johns' jersey and held on to slow him down. While Johns was stationary, the rest of the defensemen descended on him. Meadows went straight at Johns' left knee and crashed right into it. Johns yelled loudly and fell to the ground, rolling around in pain.

The referee threw the flag, as did other officials. Johns' teammates all huddled together, other than two defensive players who went after Meadows for what they believed was a cheap shot. The officials separated the players, but the Eagle players were still yelling loudly about that is was a dirty hit.

The Eagles medical staff had rushed out to check on Johns. Dr. Douglas Morris quickly looked at Johns' knee and called for the stretcher. The doc knew that Johns could not walk or even stand. The stretcher was brought out while the medical staff was still trying to find a way to stabilize Johns and not do additional damage.

The officials had gotten together and decided to call unnecessary roughness on Meadows, and he was ejected from the game. The Eagles crowd booed as he left the field and headed to the locker room.

The game continued, and while Billy Sans played decently as the replacement, the Giants eventually won 30-23. The Eagle fans were upset and booed loudly as the Giants left the field.

While the Eagle fans were justifiably disappointed, none knew that several big-time gamblers had bet very heavily on the Giants winning. The fans also didn't know that the gamblers had paid Meadows to take Johns out of the game to increase their chances of winning.

What the gamblers didn't know was that Ben Stone, an accounting professor, and Sharon Levin, a homicide detective, would soon find themselves wrapped up in the world of illegal gambling and professional football! And when Ben and Sharon are on the case, they almost always get their man (or woman).

Chapter Two

While the game between the Eagles and the Giants was on television, Sharon and I were busy setting up our house.

We were Phillies fans and tried to go to several games during the season. We occasionally attended a Flyers game but weren't big football fans. Sure, we would watch the Super Bowl, but that was usually about it.

When we finally decided to move in together officially, we had several things to take care of. We had to finish some work at Sharon's house in South Philly. Her roof was rather old, so she had a roofer replace it. She needed some work done in the kitchen, including getting a new refrigerator and gas stove. There was a lot of painting she wanted to be done, and we thought about doing it together, but neither of us was very handy, so we paid some local painters. Once we got her place looking presentable, we put it on the market.

It only took a week for it to sell at a reasonable price. However, the new owner wanted to move quickly, so we had to get Sharon's stuff either moved into my place, sold, or into storage. Sharon had been living a lot in my home for a number of years, so she didn't feel that many of her things needed to be moved to my place. She decided to sell a lot of her furniture, and what she couldn't sell, she donated to Habitat for Humanity. She got a small storage locker for a few pieces of memorabilia, but there wasn't much.

We decided we already had most of the furniture we would need at my place. Sharon had a couple of chairs that had some fond memories, so we found a place to put them. I already had two nicely laid out bedrooms, so we didn't need any more. Sharon had a few pictures she wanted to keep, so I had to sacrifice some to make room for her things. To be honest, it was not that much of a loss. In fact, I was happy to get rid of them.

We had just sat down for Indian dinner with some Hoegaarden beer. I said, "So, do you feel like we have made much progress on bringing our houses into just one?"

"I do. Having lived most of the time with you at your place for the past few years certainly made it much easier."

"Do you miss your place down in South Philly?"

"A little, but not that much. My place was pretty nice, but it wasn't Rittenhouse Square, so this is a nice upgrade. Plus, this house is closer to a lot more restaurants, bars, and nightlife locales. We've been going out a lot of late, so it's not like I missed very much, but it is very comfortable to be closer to things."

"So, how do you feel about officially living together?"

"Funny you should ask. My father called me yesterday and asked me that exact question. And I'll give you the same answer I gave him: I think it's great. In fact, I'm somewhat surprised how much this change has impacted my feelings about us. I can't explain it, but I have stronger feelings about you than I had before. How about you?"

"Same thing! And I, too, am somewhat surprised. We have been together for a good while, and at first, I didn't think moving in together would have much of an effect, but I was wrong. It just feels like we took another step toward our relationship growing. Really caught me off guard, but I'm happy with the feeling."

"So, since we took that step of moving in, what do you think should be the next phase?"

That caught me off guard, and I wasn't sure what to say to Sharon. I went with the truth and said, "I can't say that I know. I guess the next step would be getting married, but I don't know how you feel about it, and I'm not sure that I know either."

Sharon smiled, "I don't know either. As you know, I've never felt like I had to be married. I grew up in a very traditional family, and all my siblings are married with kids. But the fact that everyone has gone the traditional way, I've never felt any pressure about conforming to societal norms. Not that I'm against them, but I'm pretty happy with the life we have carved out for now. It's also funny that my mother gave a talk many years ago telling me I didn't have to get married and have kids. She just wanted me to be happy, and if I didn't follow the standard route, she was okay with that."

I said, "My mom and dad said the same thing to me. As you know, I was an only child, but there are plenty of nieces, nephews, and like. Lots of Stones around North Carolina and a few other places, so I don't have to save the Stone name from extinction."

"So, I guess we are doing okay right now, and we don't need to have any serious life-changing discussions right now."

"Well, it wouldn't be life-changing, but I was wondering if we should take a special trip somewhere to celebrate our new stage of life. Got any interest?"

"I think that's a great idea! Got any ideas of where you would like to go?"

I smiled and said, "I know you have never been there, but I've been to Maine a few times and found it interesting. Find a place by the ocean and curl up with good books, food, and sex."

Sharon laughed and said, "Okay, that is a bit of a surprise, but you come up with some interesting places to go. Funny, I thought we should return to Malta and not get involved in cryptocurrency and the mob. Maybe we could go over during Carnival, which is supposed to be fun."

I put my arm around Sharon and said, "What the hell? We should do both! Since you sold your house, we certainly have the money, so let's just splurge a little. Pick a week for Maine sometime before it gets too cold, and then plan to go over to Malta during Carnival. I know that Carnival is in late February this year, so that I can put my classes online for the week, and we can hit the road."

Sharon leaned over some more and said, "I like where things are headed right now, Stone."

"So do I."

Little did we know that our lives would get more complicated soon.

Chapter Three

Dr. Morris had known almost instantly that Franklin Johns had sustained a severe injury. Likely an anterior cruciate ligament or ACL tear. The doctor and the medical staff immobilized Johns to limit any additional damage. Johns was moved into the ambulance and then transferred to Penn Medicine's emergency room in West Philadelphia.

Johns was moved from the ambulance into the emergency room triage area. From there, an ER nurse, Ryan James, checked Johns' vital signs, which were pretty decent. His blood pressure was up, but that was expected, given how much pain he was in. He had sustained a severe injury to his knee, but no open wounds or blood poured from around his knee. From his experience, Ryan knew that Johns was in great pain, but pain meds couldn't be administered until an ER doctor gave the okay.

Just 15 minutes later, the ER doctor, Lynda Murray, entered the triage room. She asked Ryan, "So, where are we?"

Ryan responded, "This is Franklin Johns, a running back for the Eagles. He took a tough hit on his knee and collapsed—probably an ACL tear. The Eagles doctor stabilized the knee, and Johns was rushed to us. The only thing I have done so far is check his vitals. BP is up, but otherwise, he's not in bad shape. The Eagles doctor decided to wait on any pain meds until Johns got to the hospital."

Dr. Murray said to Johns, "Well, Mr. Johns, on a scale of 1 to 10, what would you consider how much pain you are in?"

Johns replied in a whispered voice, "Can I say an 11?"

"Somehow, I thought you might say something like that," responded Murray. "I will get you some morphine to help with the pain. It will take a few minutes to kick in but not that long. Then I will test your knee and see what I need to do right now to make you as comfortable as possible."

Dr. Murray got a hypodermic needle and gave Johns the shot of morphine. Then she had him sit on the bed so she could remove the brace Dr. Morris put on his knee. She could tell where the damage was most acute as she tested different parts of his knee. Johns sometimes squirmed and even yelped at some of the doctor's manipulations. It was clear to Dr. Murray that Johns had a sprained ligament at the least and maybe more.

Dr. Murray said, "So, as I'm sure you already know, you have had some serious knee damage. You might have an ACL tear, but it might only be a sprain. I will get you another wrap to immobilize you as much as possible. Then we will find a bed upstairs and get you as comfortable as possible. The attending orthopedic surgeon will likely order an MRI as soon as possible. The surgeon is great so you will be in good hands."

Johns inquired, "What's the surgeon's name?"

"Dr. Stephen Bagley. He's done a ton of surgeries similar to what you likely will need. Once we get you upstairs, I'll have him come in to introduce himself. They may be able to get you in for the MRI early tomorrow. It's pretty late in the day to get one done today."

"Doesn't look like I'm going anywhere soon," chuckled Johns.

"No, I think you'll be around for a while," said Dr. Murray.

Johns asked, "Since I was in the ambulance and the ER, I never heard if we won. Do you know?"

"I don't know, but let me check with Ryan." She stepped around the corner and said, "Ryan, did the Eagles win?"

"Sorry to say, but no, they lost 30-23. Really tough fourth quarter."

Johns said, "That's just great. I tear my knee apart, and we lose the game. Maybe the morphine will help my mood as well as my pain."

Dr. Murray said, "I'm not much of a football fan, but I know the Eagles have been playing pretty well. Sorry, you lost, but even more sorry you tore up your knee."

"Goes with the job," said Johns.

Murray smiled. She had another wrap that was sturdier for Johns' knee. He jerked a few times as she adjusted his knee, but the morphine kicked in, so he was in less pain. After she got him correctly set up, Ryan and another nurse helped Johns into a wheelchair. Dr. Murray tested how Johns fit in the wheelchair and made the last few adjustments.

She told Johns, "I think you are about as stable as we can make you. I just got notified that a room is available on the third floor. Ryan will help you get up there and get you settled. There is not much more that I can do now except wish you the best of luck in your recovery. As I'm sure you already know, it will take a while, but many people recover from such an injury. And Dr. Bagley is one of the best orthopedic surgeons around. He will take good care of you."

"Thanks, Doc. Appreciate your taking such good care of me. Once I get back up and running, I'll get you some Eagles tickets. You said you're not a big fan, but it's still a great way to spend a Sunday afternoon. Particularly if we win!"

"I appreciate the offer. Again, I wish you the best of luck in your recovery."

Ryan took Johns up in the elevator to the third floor. He moved Johns in, and another nurse helped get Johns situated in his room. Johns decided to lean back and try to find a comfortable spot. Ryan showed Johns how to use the TV and the call button. After he gave Johns a few more instructions, Ryan wished him the best of luck, and he and the other nurse left the room.

Johns decided to watch a little of the Sunday night game. It was the Chiefs and the Broncos. Johns didn't care much about the game because the Eagles weren't playing either team this season unless the Eagles ended up meeting one of them in the Super Bowl. Johns only smiled and thought, boy, wouldn't that be a treat.

After about 45 minutes, a man with a white doctor's coat entered. "Hi, I'm Dr. Stephen Bagley. I'm an orthopedic surgeon, and I'm going to be the one who will be doing your surgery." Bagley reached for Johns' hand.

As they broke their handshake, Johns said, "Nice to meet you, doc, but obviously in better circumstances."

"Yeah, I know that you play for the Eagles. Sorry about your injury. I saw a replay, which was pretty brutal."

"It was a cheap shot. The guy who hit me knew I was being held in place, and he went straight for my knee—nothing I could do to get out of the way. I heard a few of my teammates got after the guy. I hope they knocked him around pretty good."

Bagley replied, "Well, mostly we need to figure out how badly you were injured. I've got you scheduled for an MRI tomorrow morning. Once I get a look at the films, I'll know better where we are."

"Just counting on you to do the best to get me back on the field."

"I've done of a lot of these types of surgeries. Don't worry; I'll get you back up and running as soon as possible."

Dr. Bagley knew everything to do regarding the surgery but didn't know that he would soon be threatened to keep Johns off the field as long as possible. That wasn't something he had ever studied in medical school.

Chapter Four

Frank Welborn, John Forman, and Ronnie Edwards were big-time sports gamblers who rarely visited Vegas or Atlantic City. They did their gambling in back rooms and via the phone. The simple reason was that they didn't want to pay taxes. If they won enough money in either Vegas or Atlantic City, they would have to pay taxes, and they didn't have any interest in doing that. Plus, they knew they would be winners if they managed their gambling by balancing their bets. Maybe not be big-time winners, but they would still make money. But sometimes, they would take a big chance to bring in the big bucks. However, they had to take steps to ensure they would be winners. Thus, they paid Len Meadows $50,000 to ensure that Franklin Johns was not on the field when the game was on the line.

In addition to gambling, the three were always on the lookout for other arrangements to bring in more ill-gotten gains. They had decided to set up an accounts payable scheme to siphon off some money from the Linc. They worked with the head accountant who handled the bills there. All the accountant needed to do was set up fake invoices paid by Aramark, who managed all the food at the Linc. The accountant got a piece of the action, and Welborn, Forman, and Edwards took the rest. They had been doing it for years and averaged about $20,000 per Eagles game. Between their two scams, the three were doing very well financially.

The trio met to have lunch at Ralph's Italian Restaurant in South Philly. They all ordered the lasagna, which was considered Ralph's best dish. They ordered a bottle of Merlot to share. They had much to celebrate!

Welborn said, "So, fellas, why don't we have a toast? We made over $200,000 on the Eagles game. Got to be one of our biggest wins ever."

Forman smiled and said, "Yep, we did great, but I gotta admit I was getting worried in the third quarter. It didn't seem like we would have an opportunity to take out Johns. That dumbass linebacker took way too long to get Johns off the field."

"I was getting a bit nervous, too," said Edwards. "But it worked out, and we made a ton of dough."

As they toasted to their success, Welborn said, "So, do you guys think we should have one bigger score before the end of the regular season? I'm sure Johns will be out for a while, so maybe we should focus on the Eagles and their backup running back, Billy Sans."

Edwards said, "Johns is better than Sans, but Sans is pretty decent. Plus, why don't we pick another game to bet on other than an Eagles game? Lots of games to choose from."

"But that is going back to looking at the overall odds just like every other gambler," replies Welborn. "If we're going to make one more oversized bet, we must ensure we will win. We must take the 'gambling' out of the equation and be certain of the outcome."

Edwards said, "So, which game do you like, and how do you think we can surely win? You know that there are a lot of guys out there trying to do the same thing, so how are we going to make sure we are the winners?"

"First thing I think we should do is wait to see how injured Johns is," Welborn replied. "It looked like a serious injury, but we must be sure he is out for the season. I don't think he will return, but we must avoid the Eagles if he recovers quickly. That guy is talented, and we don't want him on the field."

Edwards said, "I asked around with some of the workers at the Linc, and I heard that Johns is having an MRI tomorrow morning. Do you think he can come back before the season ends?"

"As I said, I think we need to be sure. We'll sit tight for a few days and inquire about Johns' situation. If he is out for the rest of the season, we can ride the wave with Sans and put down a big bet. In fact, the Giants game up at MetLife Stadium would be a good one to use as a big bet try. If Sans is still the only running back, then our odds on the Giants winning would likely be good."

"So, you think we should just sit tight right now and see about the prognosis for Johns?" said Forman.

Welborn smiled and said, "Prognosis! Wow, I didn't know you could use such big words. Yeah, we sit tight for now. We don't have to decide anything today. Just have a little Merlot and some lasagna."

Forman smiled and said, "Plus, the money we are making with our accounts payable scheme down at the Linc is going well. With all the fake invoices running through Aramark's accounting system, we are bringing in almost $20,000 in additional funds from an Eagles game. Between that scheme and our gambling, we are having a hell of a year. Keep those two operations running, and we can retire from breaking the law for a while. Just travel down to the islands someplace and take it very easy."

The three gamblers toasted their success one more time. They were sure they could make at least one more big bet while Johns was out. Combined with the accounts payable scam, it would be a hell of a year for them.

They didn't know that Stephen Bagley was a very talented orthopedic surgeon. If there was any surgeon who could get Johns back on the field in the least amount of time, Bagley was a clear choice. But Bagley just figured that his job was to provide the best possible medical care that he could provide. However, he didn't know things would get much more complicated than just knee surgery. Doing knee surgery was going to be the easiest part of his job!

Chapter Five

The following day while Johns got ready for an MRI at 10 a.m., I was concluding an executive education seminar at Aramark on evaluating how goodwill should be used to assess the Economic Value-Added analysis results. My original academic research was just another paper, and I figured only a handful of academics would read it. However, it got picked up by some practitioner journals. AB InBev even hired me to analyze that company's EVA calculation in Leuven, Belgium. It was great that Sharon and I got a trip to Belgium out of the work even though we were also accosted by the mobsters while in Belgium—just another overseas trip filled with drama. Anyway, I am still getting some mileage out of the paper because of all the notoriety. One of the senior accountants at Aramark had read about the article and saw that I was in the area, which led to the seminar I was finishing.

I had about 20 participants from Aramark's senior accounting staff. It was early, but they all seem interested in what I had to say. It certainly helped that I knew EVA calculations figured prominently in their compensation calculations.

"As we saw, goodwill can significantly determine the EVA calculation. Goodwill can substantially impact how a company employs EVA to determine executive compensation. I hope you found my presentation valuable, and I appreciate your attendance at this seminar. Thank you!"

There was a round of applause as everyone stood up. Michael Samuel was the senior accountant who set up this seminar. He came over to shake my hand and said, "Ben, that was very interesting.

You made a strong case that goodwill is important for the EVA calculation. And since our compensation depends on an EVA analysis, it greatly benefits us. Thanks so much for your insight."

"Michael, happy to help. I was impressed with how engaged your participants were. It's early in the day, but they seemed interested in my paper. I've done a few executive seminars and the participants sometimes don't put their phones down."

Samuel said, "That sometimes happens, but I encourage our participants to keep their heads in the game. It doesn't always work, but you are a very engaging speaker, which helped a lot. Also, your seminar focuses on how much money people will receive with their bonuses, so they certainly have a vested interest in what you say. That surely helps."

I smiled and said, "It's quite true that bonus time can play a significant role in how my presentations go with this topic. Anyway, thanks again for the opportunity to present. Hope you find that my approach is useful in your analyses."

"Ben, I have another issue I want to discuss with you. Do you have a few minutes? Maybe we could go get some coffee and have a short chat?"

"I've got some time. I don't have a class until later this afternoon, so I'm happy to have a coffee."

"There is a Starbucks around the corner. Why don't we head over there? I'm sure we can find a quiet place to talk."

Samuel and I headed out to the local Starbucks. I got a black coffee while Samuel decided on a café latte. We found a seat by the corner where no one was close by. We took our places, and Samuel began.

"So, Ben, what I want to discuss with you has nothing to do with EVA. We seem to have a problem with some accounts payable fraud at the Linc. Do you have time to help us figure out what's going on?"

I was quite surprised about Samuel's query. I knew that he was a CPA and that Deloitte was Aramark's outside accountant, so he had a lot of top-shelf accounting talent at his disposal. Hard to figure out why he would need my help, but I said, "I can probably make some time, but why would you need my assistance? You have more than enough accountants on your staff, so I don't know what I could bring to the party."

"You're right that we have a large number of accountants on staff and all the resources of Deloitte, but this one is a bit tricky. We think some accounts payable fraud is happening with the Linc, but we're concerned because we don't know who is doing it. I decided to ask you for help since I am quite sure you are completely independent, and if anything shady is going on, you will try very hard to uncover it."

I replied, "But the operation at the Linc must be huge. Can only one accountant handle that much data?"

"We already have gathered all the accounts payable information for the last year into an Excel spreadsheet. You will be looking for any anomalies in how the data lays out. It's quite possible you won't find anything, but we can compensate you well for looking. What do you say?"

"I'll give it a look. I can't turn down an exciting consulting gig that pays well!"

While I was convinced to accept some consulting work, Dr. Bagley had already gotten the MRI back for Johns, and the results were as expected. Johns had an ACL sprain, but it wasn't a tear.

Bagley took the elevator up to Johns' room. He entered the room and said, "Well, Mr. Johns, I have some good news. Yes, as we thought, you have an ACL injury in the left knee, but it's not as bad as we thought. It is a grade 2 sprain, not a tear. You might return before the season ends. That's good news, I would think."

"That is great news, Doc. Do I have to have surgery? Any way to get my knee fixed without the knife?"

"Sure, we could go that way, but I'm pretty sure that if you want to get back on the field, letting me clean up your knee makes that recovery more likely. Without surgery, I seriously doubt that you would get back before the end of the season."

Johns said, "So I go under the knife tomorrow?"

"Yep, first thing. I've got you scheduled for 8 a.m. It will only take about 90 minutes, and you'll be out from anesthesia before noon. Then it's time to start talking about rehab. We have some of the best rehab experts in the city, so we'll take outstanding care of you. I'll know more when I see your knee tomorrow, but I think you might get back in a month or six weeks. That wouldn't happen if I didn't clean the knee out some."

Both Bagley and I figured that this was, in many ways, just another day at the office for both of us. Little did we know that we would soon be involved with some big-time Philly gamblers, and we would both be physically threatened!

Chapter Six

Dr. Bagley arrived at the hospital at 6:00 a.m. Surgeons usually get a head start on their day, particularly if they have more than one procedure. Dr. Bagley had Johns up first, and then he had another ACL to do in the early afternoon. The second one was a complete tear, so he knew that would take longer. He still figured he would be done by 4 p.m., a typical surgery day.

The anesthesiologist on duty was Dr. Andrea Brooks. She had worked with Bagley many times, and each knew how the other worked. They had a shorthand means as to how each one did their jobs. Dr. Brooks was also early as she had to assemble all the meds needed for the surgery. She would have Johns under the initial sedation by 6:30 a.m. and leave him entirely by 7:30 a.m.

Bagley had a couple of surgical residents who were coming to watch the procedure. In addition, he had his favorite nurse, Liz Heisler, who would assist in the surgery. Like Dr. Brooks, Heisler had worked with Bagley many times, and if she was available, Bagley always requested her for the OR.

Johns had already been taken over to the OR. Bagley wanted to talk to him briefly before Brooks put him under for the initial anesthesia. He said to Johns, "So this is your day. Don't worry, as I have done hundreds of procedures like this. As I said, we should have you back in recovery before noon. A couple of hours there, and then we've got a room already waiting for you."

Johns said, "Sounds great, Doc. Considering this injury could have been much worse, I'm positive things will come out well. But do I have to eat the Jell-O that they always have at the hospital?"

Bagley smiled, "No, not if you don't want to. We'll get you a fruit cup or something. However, I've got to say that the food here at Penn is pretty decent. Not something from Ruth's Chris Steak House, but a definite improvement over what we used to have."

"Sounds good. Do a good job."

"We plan to."

Johns was moved into position in the OR. Brooks gave him his first sedation, and he nodded out. As Brooks gathered her other drugs to keep Johns under for the procedure, Bagley had a brief discussion with his residents.

"So, folks, as you know, this is a pretty straightforward procedure. It's a grade 2 sprain. We'll make three incisions over Johns' knee. We'll open him up to get to the ligament, and then I will reattach it so it is back in the appropriate spot. Since it wasn't torn, I don't have to replace the ligament."

One of his residents, Dr. Robert Massey, asked, "Was it necessary to do the surgery? Couldn't he have gone through rehab without the cutting?"

Bagley smiled and said, "Maybe, but since we are cutters, we want to cut. Seriously, it is possible that he could have recovered without the surgery, but cleaning up his knee by cutting will probably reduce his time to recovery. As you probably know, Johns is a star running back for the Eagles, and if there is some way to get him back onto the field before the season ends, that's what Mr. Johns would like to happen."

Bagley's other resident, Dr. Warren Bills, asked, "Are we only going to watch, or are we going to get our hands dirty?"

Bagley thought to himself: Just like when I was a resident. I want to get to do it, not just watch it. He said, "I will open him up and maneuver his ligament. Once I have that, I'll let you two draw straws on who gets to close. It's straightforward, but you can never get enough practice, even with the simple things."

Both residents smiled at each other. They both wanted to close, so they each wanted to win their little bet.

Johns was entirely under anesthesia by 8:30 a.m. Bagley and the rest of his team gathered around. Everyone knew their jobs, so it took no time to get started.

Bagley opened up the knee and quickly assessed if what he had seen with the MRI was what he saw in front of him. It was, so he knew he did not need to take a piece of tendon from another body part, as is usually the case. A new device recently developed called a WasherCap would be used to support the ligament. It was minimally invasive and easily placed in the injured knee. It only took about 45 minutes for Bagley to put the cap into position, and the only thing left was to close up the knee.

Bagley said, "Okay, gents, you two must choose who will close. We don't have any coins available, so you two can do rock, paper, scissors. Best of three."

Massey and Bills both smiled. The first time Massey went rock while Bills went scissors—one for Massey. The second time Bills went paper, and Massey stayed with rock. One all. Third round, Massey stayed with rock a third time, and Bills went scissors. Massey won and showed a little smile on his face. Bagley smiled and said, "We have at least 50 years of higher education in this room, and we're making decisions with rock, paper, scissors." He couldn't help but chuckle.

Massey only took about 30 minutes to close Johns. He was moved from the operating table onto a gurney and was wheeled away. He was transferred to recovery and would probably start coming out of anesthesia soon. Bagley didn't have much time before his following procedure was scheduled, but if Johns weren't awake, Bagley would have Liz give Johns the excellent news that the surgery went well and that he could start his recovery soon.

Johns and Bagley didn't know that there were some hiccups in that plan named Welborn, Forman, and Edwards. The three gangsters would not be happy that Bagley would have Johns up and about very quickly. They weren't going to be satisfied at all!

Chapter Seven

Dr. Bagley didn't get to talk to Johns before his next operation, but Liz told the player that things had gone well. Johns had been in recovery for about three hours, then moved to a private room on the fourth floor.

Bagley wasn't doing surgery today, so he had plenty of time to see Johns. He got to Johns' room at about 10 a.m. Johns was awake and watching sports. That wasn't much of a surprise.

Bagley came in and said, "So you look to be doing pretty well here, Mr. Johns." They shook hands.

"I'm doing okay. Stiffness in my knee, but that's not too surprising. But more importantly, how do you think it went?"

"The sprained knee was exactly as I thought it would be based on the MRI. As we discussed, you might have just gotten away with rehab but wouldn't have returned before the season's end. So, we installed a new device called a WasherCap to help support your knee. Overall, we made your knee more stable, which will minimize the likelihood that you will be reinjured. No promises on that, but I think you made the right decision to have the surgery."

"When do I leave the hospital and start the rehab trek?"

"You should stay in the hospital for another two days. Once you get home, we'll set you up with a rehab schedule."

Johns said, "That sounds great. Just so you know, the team doctor, Dr. Morris, would like to meet with you this afternoon. Dr. Morris is a great guy, and he has been working with the Eagles for years, so he's been around many football injuries. I'm sure he's seen ACL sprains a lot."

"That sounds fine. I'm only doing office visits today, so I have some free time, and I'm sure I can work him in. But I would like to be the lead dog on this rehab since I'm the one who did the surgery."

"Don't worry. Dr. Morris has seen many football injuries but relies on specialists to make the final medical decisions. He will not get in your way with what you want to do. He's a great guy. He's not even that big of a football fan, but he likes being around the locker room. By the way, have you ever done any surgery on athletes before?"

"No one who would be considered famous. I got a few local tennis players and golfers who needed work, but no one you would consider famous. Well, at least until you came through the doors."

Johns laughed and said, "Well, if I can get back onto the field in record time, maybe you can pick up a new line of business."

Bagley smiled and said, "I would likely get swamped but having a famous athlete as a patient would be pretty cool. I played some squash in college, but we didn't have a team. Just had some guys who hung out and played some when we had time."

"Not a sport I am familiar with, but having something to play is good. Certainly, you can break the monotony when studying all the time. I was the starting running back for Penn State, so I had little time to study during the fall. But I studied when I could," Johns laughed out loud.

Bagley laughed and said, "Well, if I were relying on my athletic prowess to pay my bills as you are, I would be pretty much broke. Anyway, I've got to run. Tell Dr. Morris to have me paged when he gets here, and I'll try to make some time to talk."

"Sounds great, Dr. Bagley! And thanks again for fixing my knee."

"It's in my job description."

Bagley went back to making his rounds with his other patients. At about 2 p.m., he got buzzed on his phone and was told that the doctor for the Eagles was available if Bagley had time. He told the receptionist he could meet Dr. Morris in about 15 minutes. Bagley gave the receptionist his office number so Morris could wait.

Bagley went to his office and saw a middle-aged man waiting outside his office. Bagley came over, extended his hand, and said, "Dr. Morris, I assume?"

"Call me, Doug. Thanks for taking the time to talk about how Franklin is doing."

Bagley pointed to his office and directed him to sit down. Bagley said, "So, I guess you know about the surgery I did yesterday?"

"I do. It sounds like Franklin did okay. Sprain versus a tear is great news."

"It could have been much worse. As the doctor for the Eagles, I'm sure you have seen some nasty injuries."

"I won't bore you with all of them, but yes, it's a tough sport. Hardly a game goes by that I don't have to have a look at someone. But ACLs are all too common, and as you know, a severe tear could put a player out to pasture. At the least, a severe tear could take nine months to a year, trying to rehab. Franklin was fortunate. Anyway, what would you recommend we do?"

"It's rehab, rehab, rehab, but you know that. I'm sure you know we have some of the best rehab specialists in the city, if not the country. And I'm sure you also know there is no magic to getting Johns back and able to play. Steady rehab, try not to push him too hard, and then see what happens. Since Johns is an athlete, I'm guessing he quickly recovers from injuries."

Morris replied, "To be honest, this is the first serious injury that Franklin has had. Hard to believe he played four years at Penn State and five years with the Eagles, and he has only had a few relatively minor injuries. He had a couple of bad sprains and one or two bad muscle tears in his legs, but he always was able to get back on the field in less than a week. The kid has great recovery ability. Always has been able to."

Bagley said, "Sounds like you've got it well in hand. The only thing I can offer is good luck. He's a nice guy, and I wish him the best."

"Thanks. I'll keep you informed on how he is doing. And I appreciate how much attention you gave him. I've had doctors working on members of the team who didn't care about the player, just getting the job done. You spent some extra time with Franklin, and I appreciate it."

They shook hands, and Bagley returned to his rounds. Again, just another day, except one of the orderlies overheard what was said. He knew some unsavory guys who might pay to have some inside information about the Eagles.

Certainly, it might be worth a shot!

Chapter Eight

While Sharon didn't have an active murder case, she always had paperwork to do. Plus, she had recently been chosen to do a one-day seminar on money laundering since she and I had spent a lot of time on that subject. She presented to about 20 members of the force what to look for in money laundering.

Meanwhile, I was in my office at Temple trying to get started on the Aramark project. Michael Samuel provided me with a computer stick with all the data for the Linc's revenue numbers for the most recent year. One of the first things I knew I needed to do was conduct an analysis using Benford's Law.

Benford's Law dates back to 1881, when a Canadian-American, Simon Newcomb, found that a large set of numbers could be plotted to determine their distribution. He found that by using a logarithmic scale, the distribution could be determined, and by having the distribution, he could uncover if that distribution was random or if it had been manipulated. Newcomb was an astronomer who focused on physics and math, but Benford's Law was helpful in elections, criminal cases, and even macroeconomic analysis. But for my purposes, Benford's Law would be applied to accounts payable fraud. If the accounts payable distribution was incorrect, there was likely some fraud.

I had a large dataset to convert into Microsoft Excel files with which I could plot the distribution. It took a while to format the data into what I needed, and I ran it through Excel. It became apparent that there had been some manipulation of the data. That was a clear suggestion of fraud.

Then the next question was how the fraud was being perpetrated. What was being done down at the Linc that led to the scam? There were several options, but the most straightforward method was to have fictitious invoices. But I had thousands of invoices, so how could I determine which ones were real or fake? Then I had a lightbulb moment because I remembered a movie called The Accountant.

The movie starred Ben Affleck and Anna Kendrick. In the film, Affleck had high-functioning autism and was a math savant. His math skills had been used to launder money for various mob members. But the scene that I remembered was one where Affleck was explaining how he could find out there was fraud in the company he was examining. He told Kendrick that people tend to use the same numbers repeatedly when they are faking numbers. In the movie, because he found similar numbers over and over, he suspected there was fraud.

I'm not a savant regarding math, but I'm not that bad. I reworked the computer files and examined them to see if any invoices seemed unusual. Since The Linc has 61 different food vendors, a lot of money moves around. It would take a while to distinguish between the actual invoices and the fakes. But I felt I had made decent progress even on my first run at the data. If I could keep it up, I might have some results to report in just a few days. But I also know that the best-laid plans don't always work out.

While I was looking at the data, the gamblers, Welborn, Forman, and Edwards, were finding out some bad news regarding the Eagles. The orderly who heard about Johns and his recovery time had passed the info to some local small-time gamblers. The info made the rounds among gamblers in the Philly area until it finally reached Welborn.

He got off the phone, turned to his two partners, and said, "Okay, we may have a problem."

Forman said, "Great. What is the problem?"

"I was on the phone with a guy who had heard Johns' injury wasn't as bad as we thought. He heard Johns might return to full strength in less than a month."

Edwards said, "So that means we must pick different games to bet on. It's no big deal."

"It is a big deal because we were counting on Johns being out for the rest of the season. If he's going to be back, that changes the likelihood that the Eagles will lose," said Welborn.

"But all the gamblers, here and even in Vegas, know who is playing and who is not. We don't have that much of an advantage over all the other players," said Forman.

Welborn replies, "Yeah, but we have some inside information about Billy Sans, the backup running back. I was counting on us having him in the game. If Johns returns, our odds of the Eagles losing will drop a lot. And we counted on the Eagles losing a game to be our last big score for the football season. Make a killing and then lay low for a while."

Edwards asked, "So what do you think would help us out some?"

Welborn thought for a moment and smiled. "We need to convince the doctor who did Johns' surgery that Johns isn't ready to play. If we can get him to tell the team doctors that Johns should stay out for the rest of the season, then our odds go back up for a big score."

"So, we will convince an orthopedic surgeon to lie about Johns' injury and keep Johns out of commission. Why would the doc do that?" inquired Forman.

"Because we'll get a couple of knee busters to call on the doc. The doc is probably not tough, so we twist him a little, and he'll do what we want."

Forman and Edwards both smiled. They nodded, and Forman said, "Sounds like a plan to me."

Welborn said, "I know just the guys we can get to muscle the doc. Couple of guys from Northeast Philly. I'll check in with them tomorrow morning."

The gamblers didn't know Dr. Bagley was a little tougher than they thought. But they would find out soon enough.

Chapter Nine

L en Meadows had been pleased about getting the $50,000 for the hit he laid on Johns, but he was getting a bit nervous that someone might find out what he had done. When he decided to take the money, he figured it was easy. But he had recently thought there was a chance that he could be found out. On the one hand, he thought his best plan was to keep quiet, but he felt he needed to talk to someone. One of his close friends on the team was a safety named Fred Harris. He had decided to spring for lunch with Harris to lay out what had happened, and he wanted to get some advice on what he should do, if anything.

Meadows invited Harris to a Jewish deli in North Jersey. Meadows got to lunch early and had a cup of coffee. As he was finishing his first cup, Harris arrived. Meadows had picked a table far from anyone so they could speak candidly.

Harris came to the table, put out his hand, and said, "Len, thanks for the offer for lunch. I've never been to this place but heard it is great." They exchanged handshakes.

Meadows replied, "Glad you were able to make it. Why don't we check out the menu first, and then we can chat?"

Harris nodded and agreed. The waiter came over, Meadows refilled his coffee, and Harris ordered coffee. When the waiter returned, both players had decided on their orders. Meadows selected a Reuben sandwich, while Harris ordered a cheeseburger and fries. After the waiter left, both sat back and smiled at each other.

Harris said, "So you had a decent game with the Eagles. Great that we were able to come back and win. Sorta sucks that Johns got hurt, but that's just part of the game."

"That's what I wanted to talk to you about. Johns is a good guy, and I feel pretty guilty that he got injured."

"Fred, it just happens. I was getting retaped when it happened, so I didn't see it until it was on TV. Rough hit, but it happens. Rarely do we play a game with no one getting injured. But you were a little late getting to him, and you could have gone lower on his leg to take him down. He might still have been injured, but probably not gotten an ACL hit."

Meadows replied, "So I wanted to talk to you. Can I count on you to keep this to yourself?"

"Sure, we are teammates. We take care of each other. Why? What happened?"

Meadows lowered his head and said, "Three gamblers paid me 50 grand to hit Johns right in the knee to try to take him out."

Harris looked shocked. He said, "You mean to say you tried to take Johns out? And you got paid to do it?"

"Yeah, that's exactly what I mean. One of the gamblers got a message to me the Wednesday before the game. He told me the 50 large was mine to have. I just had to do what he asked. I hesitated for a while but contacted the gambler the next day and told him I would take the deal. I've been having money problems, so it seemed an easy decision."

"But Len, you know there is an unwritten rule that we don't go after a knee. Hell, no one would play the game if we went after knees as often as possible. We hit other body parts very hard, but the knees are off-limits. I have to say that I'm disappointed that you did that. It just ain't done."

Meadows said, "I know, and that's why I'm feeling very guilty right now. I thought I could hit and take him out but not do major damage. I don't know how Johns is doing, but I hope he's doing okay."

"Actually, I played college ball with a guy now an Eagle. I heard from him that Johns had only a sprained ACL, not a tear. He could make it back before the season is over."

"That's great news?"

"Yeah, but Len, you still pulled a dirty trick out there. As I said, we play hard but don't try to hurt people because it will come back to bite us in the ass. I think you need to do something to make amends for this. You can't just shut your eyes and hope it goes away."

Meadows said, "I know. I need to do something but don't know what to do. I just needed the money, but I feel bad about what I did."

"Well, you did this for the money, but I think you could donate some of the money you got to a charity. I know the Eagles have several charities, and you could send some that way."

"That's an idea, but I can't tell anyone I did it. That might be suspicious if I donate to an Eagles charity than one with the Giants."

Harris suggested, "I think you can donate some money anonymously to an Eagles charity. Johns won't know that you did it, but you will know. That's the most important thing. You try to do the right thing even if no one knows you did it. Well, only you and I will know."

Meadows thought about it and said, "Fred, I think that is a good idea. How much do you think I should donate?"

"That's up to you, but since you got 50 large for the cheap shot, it doesn't say much if you give them 100 or even 1,000 bucks. Ten grand is at least enough to help the Eagles meet some needs. I'm sure the Eagles have a charity that helps with food insecurity in the Philly area."

"10 grand? That's a lot to give up. You know I took the money because I've got money problems of my own."

Harris replied, "It's totally up to you, but you asked my opinion, so I gave it. Whatever you donate may not make you feel better, but you should at least donate something sizable. But again, your call."

"Len, thanks for talking to me. I'll give it some thought and let you know what I do. Let's have lunch."

Harris smiled and reached for his food. He felt terrible about what Meadows had done. He wasn't sure what he would do himself, but he thought he had to do something, too. He was going to have to give it some thought.

Chapter Ten

The next day, I only had one class to teach, and it was at night, so I spent more time looking at the Aramark problem. Using the Benford analysis, I had already found enough to indicate fraud. The info from the movie The Accountant also sheds some light on what might be happening.

As I sat and thought about the issues, I decided I should tell Samuel from Aramark that he needed to hire a fraud analyst because I was over my head, but I determined I should give it a little more time.

I figured the most likely way the money was being siphoned was a business email compromise. Business email compromise (BEC) was one of the most frequent means of illegally pilfering funds from a company.

I decided to read some articles about BEC. I knew a little, but I decided to do more research. After surfing the internet, I found that BEC is a sophisticated scam targeting businesses and individuals and performing fund transfers.

One of the easiest ways to run a BEC scam is for the scammers to infiltrate legitimate email accounts. Finding out such statements will allow scammers to move legal money to illegal accounts legally. Legitimate financial records and other customer accounts could be attacked, and money could be seized. I quickly focused on the list of customers that worked at the Linc with all the different vendors. Over 2,000 vendors were working at the Linc, and I knew I didn't have the skills or staff to go through more than 2,000 vendors, so I knew I would need help. Since Sharon would surely not get into this mess, I knew I would have to find other support. And then I had a lightbulb moment! I needed to call Emily Keen of the FBI.

I had already worked with Emily at the Outer Banks of North Carolina and Philadelphia, focusing on the ultra-orthodox Jewish community. I knew that I couldn't just expect Emily to burn through resources at the FBI, but since we already had developed a relationship, I figured it was certainly worth a phone call.

I looked up her phone number and called. The phone was answered with, "Keen."

"Emily. It's Ben Stone up here in Philadelphia."

"Ben, it's great to hear your voice. Hope things are going well up in Philly. How is Sharon doing?"

"Things are going pretty well up here. Sharon is doing well. She's got several cases, but not anyone that is as exciting as the Outer Banks and the ultra-Orthodox one up here. By the way, Sharon sold her house in South Philly, and we're living together in my place."

"Wow, Stone, that's a big step for you two! You going to tie the knot?"

"That will be a conversation for another time. One step at a time is what we are doing."

"That makes sense. Anyway, I always love to hear from you, but for some reason, I feel you have an ulterior motive, like a case for which you need a little help."

I replied, "I guess I'm pretty transparent. Sorry about that. I've got a new case involving the vendors who manage the Linc, our football stadium."

"I don't watch much football, but I know about the Linc. Nice place. Why, what's going on with the vendors?"

"You may know of a company called Aramark. It's one of the biggest food vendors in the country. They cover all sorts of events, including the Linc. Their chief accountant thinks some money is being pilfered from the Linc, and because of hearing about some of my consulting work, they decided to get me to look into what's happening. It's a pretty big operation, and it's way over my head to cover everything. At first, I just figured I should tell the Aramark guys to hire some fraud investigators, but at the last minute, I thought of you and that maybe you might have some ideas."

Emily replied, "Not my wheelhouse, but I know a group that might help. Have you ever heard of the Internet Crime Complaint Center? Their nickname is IC3."

"I think I saw a blurb about it on CNN. They help people and companies track down internet fraud, right?"

"That is exactly what they do! But they only really focus on internet-related crimes. IC3 is related to the FBI, and we coordinate our efforts together. Do you think your issue with the Linc is somehow linked to the internet?"

"I'm sure it is. It's a ton of data, and I know everything from invoices to sales is done through the internet. That's a great idea, but I don't know anyone at that organization."

"Fortunately for you, I do. Her name is Linda Willis. We've been involved in a couple of investigations together. She's talented and knows everything about how to examine internet fraud. I can get you a phone number or email, whichever you like."

"That would be fantastic! I know many people don't pick up their phones at the office unless they recognize the number. If you just gave me her email address, I could email her and see if she's got time to help me out."

"No problem. Her email address is lwillis@ic3.gov. Make sure to use my name."

"Emily, that is very, very helpful. I don't know where to go with this problem, so that any insight would be appreciated. On a happier note, when could you visit Philly and see the new place? Actually, it's not a new place, but it has a different layout. Sharon had a few ideas on how to change my house."

Emily laughed and said, "Yeah, I assumed she made a few changes. My schedule is tight right now, but I would love to see the new pad when I get clear. But only if you promise to one of the famous Italian restaurants in South Philly."

"Consider it done! And when I get a call back from Linda, I'll let you know. And thanks again for the help."

"No problem, Ben. And I'm looking forward to seeing both of you." With that, Emily ended the call.

I took a few minutes and sketched out what I wanted to email Linda. I wanted to give her enough information to get her attention but not so much as to overwhelm her if she was too busy to look at a lengthy idea. I was pretty sure there was enormous activity on internet fraud, and I was sure Linda was very busy. I decided on two paragraphs and sent them off to Linda. Then I waited.

As I leaned back in my chair, I decided I had made some progress today. It may not break any investigative records, but it was progressing.

I didn't know that progress was also made because the gamblers were busy finding out about other people learning about the scam they pulled during the Giants' game. At least for now, I didn't have to worry about my physical safety. Unfortunately, Len Meadows would soon discover he was not in that position.

Chapter Eleven

The gamblers, Welborn, Forman, and Edwards, got together at their favorite bar to discuss what they should do next. They had heard through the gambling hotline that Meadows had talked to a fellow player who had also passed it around to a few others. It was apparent to the three gamblers that Meadows needed to shut up and quickly.

Welborn said, "So, this dumbass football player is letting it be known about the scam we set up to stack the game in our favor. I'm not worried about the cops or the like, but other gamblers may have lost some money on that game. We need to get this guy to shut his mouth. In fact, we may need to have this guy roughed up a bit. If other gamblers find out about the scam we ran, they will not be happy. We must communicate that we weren't trying to cheat other gamblers. At least we have to make it look like that."

Forman said, "I don't know if smacking a linebacker around will make much difference. If other gamblers discover what we did, the ones who lost money will probably create many problems for us."

"You might be right," said Welborn, "but it won't hurt. Plus, if we get this linebacker knocked around, that may send a message that we are very serious players and will do what is necessary to protect the integrity of the gambling. If gamblers stop taking our bets, we'll lose a lot of money. So, anyone knows some tough guys we can pay to bash that guy around?"

Edwards replied, "I'm still not sure this is a good idea, but if you two are committed to this, the two guys I suggested to pressure the doc can also go after Meadows. Bruno Lord and Bennie Wilson.

They're from South Philly and have been around the neighborhood for years. They do a little loansharking, maybe some gambling on their own, and do some breaking and entering when they need some walking around money. I don't know them well, but they'll take any dough if I offer some."

Edwards said, "I agree that going after the linebacker is a good idea. We've got some other gamblers who will be very pissed about losing money on that game. We must send a message that we're serious about having a clean game."

"Then I'll get a message to Lord and Wilson. I don't know where they hang out, but I can make several calls. I'm sure I can get a message to them and set it up," said Welborn.

Edwards asked, "So that I know, how far are we going on this? Just a little knock around? I don't think we should hit him too hard. We don't need to have the cops involved in this thing."

"We need to make sure they don't get too carried away. I agree that we must ensure we send a message, but not involving the law is a must," said Forman.

"Then I'll get a message to these two muscle boys," said Edwards. "I'll let you know when I get it set up."

Edwards went to a coffeehouse near where he lived to get the ball running on the plan. He made a few calls and finally got a number for one of the muscle guys, Bruno Lord.

Edwards gave him a buzz, and Lord picked up. "I don't know who the fuck this is, but you better be someone I want to talk to. I'm a busy guy and don't need to be talking to marketing scammers."

"Bruno, this is Ronnie Edwards. We met a few months ago because you wanted to place a bet with me. As I recall, you won."

"Yep, I remember you, Ronnie. And yes, I won the bet. But I've got a case of the shorts with money, so I can't place any bets right now."

"Not interested in your gambling. I want to offer you an opportunity to make some cash, so if you want to bet, you'll have the dough."

Bruno chuckled and said, "That would be great. As I said, I've been having a bit of a dry run late. What do I need to do?"

"I know that you are buddies with Bennie Wilson. I need you to rough up a linebacker who plays for the Giants. We need him to keep his mouth shut about a little scam we ran a week ago. We paid the guy to put Franklin Johns out of the game. The linebacker's name is Len Meadows. I'll contact him, give him the incentive to come down our way, set up a meeting, and then you and your partner can chat with him.

"Not a problem. A linebacker is normally a pretty good-sized guy, but we've handled many situations like that. How much money do we get?"

"I'll get you five large. Pretty good pay for a conversation."

"Sounds like an easy job. Send me the address to meet him, and Bennie and I will chat with that guy. How hard do we hit him?"

"Make sure he understands what to do and not to do, but you don't need to leave any evidence. Bruise him, but not bloody him."

"Easy enough. We'll take care of it."

Edwards called Welborn and told him he had set up the plan to get Meadow's attention. He made sure to pass the information along to Forman.

Edwards sat back in his chair and reflected on how easily this had been resolved. He figured he had taken care of a little problem he and his partners had and had done it in a simple way. He didn't know what Bruno and Bennie considered bruising was not what he thought bruising was. Things were going to get out of control very soon!

Chapter Twelve

Linda from IC3 emailed me that she would happily help with my investigation. I'm sure using Emily's name got me to the top of the list. Linda said she was pretty busy until the end of the day, so we set up a time for the following day to talk about how she might be able to help. She gave me her phone number so I would know she was making the call.

The next day my meeting with Linda wasn't until after lunch, so I figured I might as well do some of my so-called real jobs as an accounting professor. It wasn't as exciting as some of my efforts with Sharon, but it was my profession.

I was again teaching an intermediate accounting class. I had 35 students in the class. Most of my students were pretty motivated, and I didn't have attendance problems, but, like every other professor in the world, I had to come up with new exams every semester. Thanks to Course Hero, Quizlet, Studypool, StudyBlue, Kahoot, and all the others like them, all of my exam materials were put up online right after I gave an exam. I missed using the test banks! You pick a textbook and get all sorts of accouterments like study guides, review materials, and test banks. Unfortunately, those days were gone.

It wasn't as big a deal for accounting professors as other disciplines because coming up with new exams each semester sometimes meant changing the numbers used in the test. I could use the test bank material many times but change the numbers the students would have to use for the tests. What I did mean was that using multiple-choice exams was pretty dead as far as accounting was concerned. I had to make up the exams and have the correct answers ready to determine the grades. Before Course Hero, the profs could use the test bank materials for some areas in the business school, marketing, supply chain, and even finance. Sadly, those days were gone.

It still made me laugh when I thought back to when I was studying accounting at The American University in DC. I used to have a professor who taught accounting theory, auditing, and business law. He always did multiple-guess exams for everything in his courses; on the surface, that was okay until I found out how he picked his exam questions.

There were several CPA review books to use to prepare for the exam. Gleim and Delaney's CPA prep book was one of the most popular at the time. My professor for all these classes told us that he used CPA prep materials for our exams at school. He suggested buying one of the older Gleim and Delaney books to prep for his class. I decided to take a chance and purchase a more recent edition. I figured it was an excellent way to prepare for my classes and get a head start on the CPA exam. I found one that was on sale at a bookstore. I still studied the textbook but used the prep classes to understand what the tests might look like.

No big deal until I sat down for the first exam in my accounting theory class. The prof used the same Gleim and Delaney materials I had bought! I barely had to read the questions. I knew the answers before finishing the question. I even pretended to be still looking at the test despite finishing it. I finished the test before any of my fellow students had even been halfway through. Perhaps more importantly, when that first test came back, I got a 96 on it, and that was because I had intentionally missed one. With the prof's curve, I scored 104 on my first one.

It was funny that the prof just kept doing it: same plan, the rest of theory, same thing auditing, and even biz law. I just kept using the Gleim and Delaney books, and I just kept getting ridiculously high grades. I felt guilty for a while, but I got over it. If the prof was so lazy to keep using the same materials, who was I to say anything? I thought it fair since the prof told us to use some out-of-date prep books.

But thanks to Course Hero and the rest, those days were long gone for accounting classes and almost all other courses. Making up exams is much more work than in the good ole days I was in school. Oh well, these times are a-changing!

At right around 1 p.m., I got a call from the number Linda had left for me. "Hello, this is Dr. Ben Stone."

"Ben, this is Linda Willis from IC3."

"Linda, thanks so much for getting back to me. I'm sure IC3 gets thousands of inquiries daily, so I appreciate your time."

"No problem. Emily Keen at the FBI and I have done some work, and she told me that you had been involved in some, how should I say it, interesting cases, including pirates in NC and ultra-Orthodox Jews in Philly. Sounds like pretty exciting stuff."

I chuckled and said, "Yeah, it has been somewhat stimulating with those things. Pretty crazy stuff for an accounting professor."

Linda snickered and said, "By the way, I am an alumna of Temple's Fox School of Business. I'm from Delaware and started at the University of Delaware but ended up at Temple because they have an excellent risk management degree. I even stuck around at Temple to get a master's degree. I thought I would end up with one of the big insurance companies, but I heard about an opportunity with IC3 and decided to grab it. I had to get additional education, but I enjoy what I do now."

"That's pretty cool that you went to Temple. Sorry I never met you here, but it is a big school."

"Yes, it is. Anyway, I've read your short synopsis of what might happen, but give me a longer rundown."

"Well, I was doing an exec ed gig for Aramark, one of the biggest food service vendors in the country. Their chief accountant told me he thought some accounts payable fraud was going down at the Linc, our football stadium. He asked me to take a look at his books. I agreed but quickly realized this would be more than a one-person operation. I got all their accounts payable info for the past two years. It's a ton of data, but I started trying to decipher what was happening. I did a Benford's analysis that indicated some manipulation of the account payable numbers. Then I started looking into business email compromise and found more indicators of possible fraud. But then I got stuck. At first, I just figured I should tell Aramark that they need to hire some fraud accountants, as there are many in the area, but then I thought of Emily and decided maybe I could do a little more before I punt the project. And that is about where I am on it."

Linda said, "Well, Ben, I have to say it sounds like you've done great work already. I can tell you where I can help. IC3 has some of the most sophisticated software to examine internet fraud. We've been at it in earnest since 2003. And yes, we get a lot of inquiries. We had over 800,000 complaints, with an estimated $7 billion in losses last year. It was a big loss. But we are always updating our analysis methods and adding new software to help curb the internet monetary loss. What I can do, if you can give me your data, is run your data through our cybercrimes software and see what I can find. Our software is very sophisticated, and we can track down a lot of internet theft. Certainly not all of it, but I can say that we can make a dent. Would that help?"

I said, "That would be fantastic! Aramark has cleared me to provide all the data I have for anyone who can assist in this venture. It's a lot of data to me but probably not much to you."

"That's probably true. Can you put all your data on sticks and send them to my office? I like to have sticks versus everything online. I guess I'm just around too much internet theft to trust it. Once I get it, I'll look at it and tell you what I can do to help. Would that work?"

"That would be fantastic! I think I will have about five sticks. It is a lot of data. Email me your address, and I will get the sticks to you by tomorrow."

Linda said, "That would be fine. I'm not sure I can jump right into your project, but I can get started soon. I have an assistant who can set up your info for our programs. I have a software manager who can run some of the initial tests for fraud. Then I can start looking for patterns to uncover what's been happening and how to stop it."

"Linda, that sounds just great. By the way, will there be a fee for doing this? I'm sure Aramark would happily pay, but I was just wondering?"

"There is no fee. We are closely related to the FBI and a governmental agency, so there is no fee. We are doing our civic duty. Protecting financial assets both here and abroad. Just get me the sticks, and I'll get us started."

I said, "Linda, that is just great news. I appreciate any help you and your team can give me. I'll get the sticks to you tomorrow. Again, thanks so much."

I hung up my phone. I sat for a minute, pondered what had been said, and then decided that having Linda involved would make this project faster. And I was even doing a job that didn't involve Sharon and the possibility of murder and mayhem. Or at least I thought there wouldn't be any murder and mayhem.

Little did I know!

Chapter Thirteen

Welborn had contacted Meadows and told him he had made much more on their bet on the Giants' game and wanted to share some spoils with him. Meadows was surprised, but Welborn told him he and his partners always tried to be fair with their gambling. They value having a good relationship with gamblers because having a reputation for honesty is good for business. Welborn told Meadows to come down to Philly to pick up his share because he was very busy with other bets. Meadows was still suspicious, but since he had donated the ten grand, as suggested by his teammate Harris, he could use the extra dough. He agreed to come down to Philly and meet Welborn at a bar on Roosevelt Boulevard in the Northeast that night.

Bruno and Bennie had told Welborn to go to The Rhawnhurst Bar and Restaurant off Castor Avenue. It was quiet most of the time, but more importantly, there was a dark backside with very few lights. Bruno knew the place well and felt that no one would hear or see anything going on if they could get Meadows outside.

Meadows left North Jersey at about 8 p.m. Edwards said he would be at The Rhawnhurst around 10 p.m. He told Meadows to meet him out back to get his money.

Meadows was still nervous about this whole thing, but the money was just too attractive not to go for it. He listened to some Nighthawks music to break the monotony of the drive. He had become a fan of the Nighthawks because he was into blues and roots music. He turned the music up because there was a lot of traffic on the Jersey Turnpike, as there usually was.

He got down to The Rhawnhurst at about 9:30, so he sat in his car, figuring he had a little time to kill. At 10 p.m., he entered the bar and returned to find Edwards. He looked everywhere but didn't see anyone. He thought it was unusual for Edwards to blow him off, but maybe something came up.

As he was getting ready to leave, a man came up behind him. The guy put a knife up to his neck. Another man came around to Meadows, who also had a knife. The fellow with a knife at Meadow's neck said, "So my friend and I need to chat with you. Don't try to do anything stupid because, as you can see, we both have knives."

Meadows did a quick assessment of the situation. He could tell he was bigger than either of these two guys, but since they both had knives in their hands, he decided it was better to play along, at least for the time being. He said, "What the fuck is happening here? I'm just supposed to meet a guy to pick up some cash. Who the hell are you?"

Bruno smiled and said, "We work with the man you will meet. He couldn't make it, so he sent us. Our job is to explain to you that there are some new developments. We are to tell you that you should stop running your fucking mouth about what happened at the Giants game. In short, stop talking to anyone about how you took a cheap shot at that running back. No more stories."

Meadows thought momentarily and said, "That's not a problem. I can easily stay out of that mess. But am I still getting the extra money?"

That was a mistake for Meadows to make. Bruno and Bennie figured this guy was expecting a lot more cash than they were, so they decided to make a point about the value of money. Bruno leaned in with his knife at Meadow's throat and said, "I gotta say I think you are making this too easy. I'm not sure we can trust you. Maybe you'll understand how serious we are if we give you a little slit of your throat."

With that, Bruno started to press down on Meadows's neck. Meadows could feel the blade going deeper into his neck, so he decided he couldn't wait to be sliced. He quickly threw his arm around Bruno, forcing the knife away from his neck.

Bruno was surprised and unprepared for Meadows to go after him. He tried to regain the advantage, but Meadows was too strong and fast. Meadows grabbed Bruno by his chest and was able to push him away. What he didn't realize was that Bennie was coming up behind him.

Bennie got a good grip on his knife and jabbed it right into Meadows's back below his heart. Meadows screamed and then toppled to the ground. Bennie's blade was still in Meadows's back.

Bruno yelped and said, "What the fuck are you doing? I think you just pierced him right in his heart."

"You asshole. I saw that guy getting the advantage against you, so I did what I had to do. The guy was going to kick your ass. What, you just wanted me to watch while you got knocked to the ground?"

"No, but I didn't want you to stab the guy. What the fuck are we going to do now?"

Bennie said, "We're going to get that knife out of that guy's back, no figure prints thank you, and then run like hell."

While Bruno and Bennie were deliberating their plan, a man came out of the bar to have a cigarette. He saw what was happening and yelled, "What the hell are you two doing?"

Bennie grabbed the knife from Meadows's back, and he and Bruno ran for their car. The bystander came over to see what was happening to Meadows. Blood was pouring out of Meadows's back. The bystander saw that the guy was in deep trouble, and he yelled for help. Two men from the bar came out, and one called 911.

Five minutes later, an emergency vehicle arrived, and both paramedics turned Meadows over to check his vitals. They were not good, and they knew they needed to get him stabilized and then quickly to an ER!

What Sharon didn't know yet, but this would soon become her problem!

Chapter Fourteen

It was very early the following day, and Sharon and I were still asleep. She was always up earlier than I was, but she had been at the office late, so she decided to stay in bed a little longer. However, Sharon always kept her phone on if she got a call from the precinct. Today was such a morning.

Her phone rang, and she picked up the phone and said, "I hope this call is important."

"Sharon, it's George Thomas, one of the cops who worked with you on the Orthodox Jewish case. Sorry to wake you up so early."

"George, what time is it?"

"5:30 a.m."

"Crap, George, why are you calling me at this time of morning?"

"My shift today started at five, so I got the call. There was a murder last night over at The Rhawnhurst Bar and Grill in the Northeast. The guy was a football player for the New York Giants. Guy's name is Len Meadows."

"How do you know it was a murder?"

"Guy was stabbed in his back. Bled out at the scene. The paramedics took the body to Penn, but he was pronounced dead on arrival. The body has already been moved to the morgue, and Dr. Durham is supposed to start the autopsy this morning. I checked in with the Chief, who said your name is at the top of the list for a homicide detective."

"Lucky for me. I assume the Crime Scene Investigation team has already been there?"

"They are over there right now. They had another murder close to the North Philly airport, so they only got to Rhawnhurst about 30 minutes ago. The bar was closed right after the attack, and a couple of uniforms kept the place clear until CSI got there. I haven't talked to them yet, so I don't know what they've found."

Sharon yawned and said, "So the Chief wants me to be in charge of this one?"

"Yep. He said if you need help, he will get you some, but I know you well, and you probably don't want anyone right now."

"I'll get over there, talk to CSI, and then decide if I need backup. I've got to shower, and then I'll come right over. And, by the way, thanks for giving me a case before the sun comes up."

"I follow the rules that the Chief sets out. Do you want me to meet you at Rhawnhurst?"

"Nah, since CSI is already there, I'm sure they have already collected a lot of evidence. If I need you, I'll give you a call. And just so you know, I know it's not your fault I'm up at 5:30. As you said, my name just came to the top of the list."

Thomas said, "Well, Sharon, maybe you can have another compelling case like the Orthodox Jewish one. Maybe even the vampire one in New Orleans that I heard about."

"I would like a normal case, but you're right that I have had some weird ones recently. Anyway, thanks, George. I'll keep you in the loop on this one since you got it started."

Sharon hung up the phone and leaned over to tap my shoulder. She said, "Ben, I'm sorry to wake you, but I have a new case, and I have to get cleaned up and head out to a murder scene."

I rolled over, stretched, and said, "What time is it?"

"It's close to 6 a.m."

"You got summoned early in the morning. Where is the scene?"

"Over at the Rhawnhurst Bar and Restaurant in the Northeast. We know it, but I don't think we have been there. The big news is that the victim is Len Meadows, a New York Giants football player. I don't know much more than that right now. Go back to sleep. I'll call you closer to your usual wakeup time of 9 a.m."

"I think you're busting my balls about my sleeping habits."

Sharon smiled and said, "Not really. If I could, I would stay in bed a little, too. Anyway, go back to bed, and I will be in touch. You don't have a class until mid-afternoon, right?"

"Nothing until 3 p.m., but I must spend some time on the Aramark case. I'm making decent progress, but I gotta keep at it."

"Well, if you stayed up, you could jumpstart your day a little earlier," chuckled Sharon.

"I could, but I'm not going to. Good luck with your case," and I rolled over.

Sharon snickered and said, "The life of an academic. Gotta love it."

Sharon showered and got dressed. She headed straight to the Rhawnhurst to catch up with the CSI team. It took about 30 minutes to get to the Rhawnhurst, and Sharon went directly to the CSI lead detective, Larry Perkins, to get his update.

Sharon stuck out her hand to Perkins, and they exchanged greetings. She said, "Good to see you again, Larry. What do you have?"

"Good to see you, too, Sharon. So far, we have pretty much exactly what it looks like. This Giants football player, a guy named Len Meadows, was stabbed from behind. It was a deep wound, and Meadows was likely bleeding very profusely. Based on what the paramedics said, the best I can tell is that Meadows dropped to the ground when he was stabbed. The blood was only found in one area near the back of the bar. I don't think Meadows even got back up after the stabbing. He might have rolled a little, but I don't think he ever got to his feet. The paramedics tried to stop the blood from pouring out, but it was a deep wound, and they knew that Meadows had already lost a ton of blood. They tried stabilizing him, but the paramedics were sure he was already gone."

Sharon asked, "Which ER did they take him to?"

"Penn."

"But there are closer ERs than Penn. Even with the lights on, the paramedics would have taken almost 30 minutes to get to Penn. Why not pick a closer ER?"

Perkins replied, "The paramedic in charge had to make a snap decision. All of the ERs that were closer than Penn were filled up. Also, the paramedic knew that if the victim were still alive, by the time the victim got to an ER, there would be a lot of work to keep this guy going. He felt that Penn had better facilities for such a significant injury. As I said, he had to make an instantaneous decision. No time to debate it. Just had to go."

Sharon said, "It sounds like it was probably the right move, even though the victim didn't make it. He probably had a better chance at Penn. Anyway, can you bring me up the speed on what evidence you have?"

"The biggest evidence is that an eyewitness emerged from the bar and saw the stabbing. Guy's name is Harold Ott. He lives close to the Rhawnhurst, one of his favorite watering holes. I talked to him for a few minutes, but Ott said he needed to go to work, but when the detectives got there, he said he would leave work and give you any details he can remember."

Sharon thought to herself that it was probably going to be a long day!

Chapter Fifteen

Sharon and I tried to have dinner together at least two nights a week. I had one afternoon class, and Sharon had to work late many nights. We had to be flexible about when to have dinner, and tonight was one of those nights.

I got home at about 6 p.m. Sharon said she would be home by about 7, so I had to figure out dinner. Since we both had had long days, it wasn't a good night to cook. We had discussed getting Indian food again because we had enjoyed it so much the last time we had it. She left it up to me to choose the food. Surprise me, she said.

I found a new Indian place called The Royal Indian Cuisine over on 20th Street. I pulled up the menu online and started to look at the choices. Right up front, I saw that they specialized in Tikki Masala, so I knew that would be one of the entrees we would share. Vegetable Samosa was always a favorite for both of us. Chicken Tikka Biryani seemed to be another one of their specialties, so I decided to go with that for Sharon.

I placed a call to the restaurant. I gave them our order and asked them to deliver it using GrubHub. I requested that it be delivered around 7:30 in case Sharon ran late, which happened frequently.

Regarding what to drink, we had water, some wine, and a few beers. It's funny how we had gone through several fancy new domestic beers and some foreign ones of late but had suddenly returned to a classic, Guinness. Sometimes simple is the best.

I had a few minutes to kill before Sharon arrived, so I looked through my latest efforts about the Linc project. I gathered all the information I had and started to put all the info on sticks to send to Linda. Since I had a little time to kill, collecting the data was a good use of my time.

While downloading all the info, I discovered I would need a few more sticks than I thought. There was a lot more than I thought I would need. Lots of data for Linda to comb through, but I was confident she had software that could process everything quickly. I knew I was fortunate that she would be able to help me. It would take me weeks to try to do it.

I heard the door open and, "Hi, honey, I'm home."

" 'Hi, honey, I'm home?' When did that start?"

Sharon laughed, "Just trying to be the good little housemate."

"So, will you cook dinner after you clean the house?"

"Not a chance in hell! I hope you already ordered something delicious."

I laughed and said, "So much for the good little housemate. Yes, we should get some Indian food delivered in about 30 minutes. Should I pour you a Guinness?"

"Both things work for me. Let's debrief on our days after we get the food. I need to decompress a little. It was a pretty tough day."

"No problem. Watch the news till the food gets here. I'm doing a little bit of work on the Linc project."

Sharon smiled and sat down in front of the TV. I got her the beer she wanted and returned to looking at the pages and pages of data that needed evaluation.

As expected, our dinner arrived via GrubHub. I tipped generously and brought the food into the kitchen. Sharon cut off the TV, came in, and helped me spread the feast. I got a Guinness for myself and another for her. We sat down to eat.

I said, "So it sounds like your day was more hectic than mine, so do you want to go first, or shall I?"

"You go first. My day may take longer, and I'm unsure where to go with my case."

"Okay, my class went fine. Students were pretty engaged, but that's probably because they have an exam next week. I got home at about 6, figured out the food situation, and then started trying to gather all the data for Linda Willis, who works at the Internet Crime Complaint Center. She wants me to send her computer sticks with the info. I thought I would only need about five, but it might take seven or eight. I can get it all done tomorrow and ship it off to her. That's about it for my day."

"The life of an academic!" she said. "You're done with your day in less than five minutes. Sometimes I wish I had spent more time in school and could have gotten a gravy job like you."

"It may seem that way, but I did have to put a lot of time into doing all that. Then I had to go through the promotion and tenure process while teaching and doing research. I have had some long days over the years, just not much right now."

"You know that I'm just kidding. I've watched you have some long, long days. Plus, thanks to you going to conferences overseas and in the US, we have had some interesting, sometimes scary, times. Have you ever talked to your colleagues at Temple about some of your adventures?"

"I have. Most don't believe me unless I show evidence of Malta, Belgium, or New Orleans. Their first take is that I'm making it all up."

Sharon smiled and said, "I know. Sometimes my fellow law enforcement coworkers think I'm making it up. People can't look at us and believe we have such exciting lives."

"Speaking of exciting, what happened with your day?"

"Well, as you know, it started very early. A linebacker for the Giants was murdered over at the Rhawnhurst Bar and Grill. Guy's name was Len Meadows. He was stabbed in the back and bled out to the ER. He was taken to Penn ER, but he was already gone."

"Well, that sucks," I said. "As you know, I don't follow football much, so the name means nothing to me. Was he a big deal?"

"He was a decent player though not a starter. He got a lot of playing time, from what I hear."

"So, what's going on with the investigation? First, how did you catch this case?"

"My name was the next on the list. It had nothing to do with knowing anyone or anything about the Giants or even the Eagles—just my turn. As far as the investigation goes, there was an eyewitness from the bar, and I went to his place of work and talked to him, but I didn't get much. It was dark, with no real lights, and the eyewitness saw two guys running behind the bar. He gave us a description, but it would apply to many guys. Not much help."

"CSI find out anything interesting?"

"Not much. A few tracks could be from the assailants, but we're unsure. The ME did his autopsy, and he couldn't find anything that might help that much. There were a lot of fingerprints in the area, but they were pretty messy, and hard to get a decent read on any of them. It's a bar and restaurant, so many people are around with fingerprints."

"Sounds like your day was less than productive."

"Quite true. Our only lead is that Meadows was ejected from the game in which Franklin Johns was injured."

"Who is Franklin Johns?"

Sharon smiled and said, "You aren't much of a football guy, are you? Very un-Philly-like of you not to know about the starting running back for the Eagles. Johns was injured during a tackle by Meadows. Referees thought it was a dirty shot and ejected Meadows from the game. According to the sports pages, Johns has an ACL strain, not a tear. Rumor is that he might make it back before the end of the season."

"And that's your big clue. An injury that occurred in an NFL game. I don't know much about football, but I have to figure that football players get injured a lot."

"I'm sure that is true, but I must go with whatever clues I might have. The only thing I have is Meadows, Johns, and the injury. I'm hoping the CSI folks can find something else, or maybe more from the autopsy, but I got what I got."

I smiled and said, "I guess both of us have some work to do."

"That we do, but for now, break open another Guinness, watch a little TV, and maybe I can think of a way to take work off our minds."

"Getting the beer right now, honey."

Chapter Sixteen

The three gamblers were not very happy. First off, they read in the newspaper that Meadows had been killed. That was not the plan. Bruno and Bennie were supposed to scare Meadows into keeping his mouth shut, not murder the guy. The gamblers were concerned that, somehow, they would be found out by the police. Welborn had been trying to get ahold of Bruno, but he hadn't had any luck yet. He guessed that Bruno was keeping a very low profile under the circumstances.

The second problem was that the gamblers had heard from the orderly at Penn that Johns might be back in action before the end of the season. They had been counting on Johns staying out of the lineup so they could place their big bet on the final game between the Eagles and the Giants up at the MetLife Stadium. There were plenty of games to bet on, but the gamblers counted on finishing their betting season with that game. The chance that Johns might come back was potentially a significant threat. They had already had some bets blow up, so to keep their customers happy, they needed to ensure this went through.

The three had huddled at their office. They knew they had to devise a solid plan to ensure the Giants' game went correctly. Welborn took the lead and asked, "So boys, what are we going to do about these flies in our ointment regarding Meadows and the Giants game?"

Forman said, "Well, there's not much we can do about Meadows. I've been asking about what the cops might know; apparently, it's not much. There was one witness, but he didn't see very much. He gave a brief description of Bruno and Bennie, but not enough that would somehow identify them. I discovered that the lead detective is Sharon Levin, a homicide cop for years. She is pretty good, but that doesn't mean she has real evidence or leads. She's been involved in some crazy ass cases, including the ultra-Orthodox case we read about in the papers. And her boyfriend is an accounting professor at Temple, so I don't think he will bring anything important to this party. Right now, I think we do not worry about that end of things. Bruno and Bennie are at least smart enough to keep their mouths shut. We need to figure out what to do with this Franklin Johns character. He's a wild card for playing in the Giants game."

"Well, we were going to have Bruno and Bennie talk to the doctor, but we changed our plan with them going after the linebacker. I guess one of us needs to have a chat with the doc. I'll volunteer, "said Edwards.

"And how will you do that? said Welborn.

"I already had the orderly we know track down this guy's schedule for the day. I know that he will be around until four this afternoon. I will take a little trip to Penn and discuss things with the doctor. Explain to him that telling the Eagles that he shouldn't play would be in his best interest."

"Wouldn't it be easier just to bribe him?" said Forman.

"Maybe, but docs at Penn probably make pretty decent dough, so I have no idea how much to offer. But I know that a threat will get his attention."

Welborn and Forman looked at each other and smiled. Welborn said, "Go for it. Just make sure to be careful. Don't let anyone hear you."

"Consider it done," said Edwards.

While Edwards and the other gamblers were plotting how to ensure Johns doesn't play, Dr. Bagley had a typical day when he wasn't operating. He had several visits with patients for whom he had done surgery. He had a kid who had torn his elbow playing football—easy surgery for Bagley. The kid would be in rehab for at least two months. Another patient, a union machinist, also had an ACL injury, but rather than strained like Johns, this one was a tear.

However, Bagley said It could have been worse. Patient might be looking at 4 to 5 months before he'd be 100%.

Bagley also met with all the orthopedic surgical staff at 2 p.m. Every two weeks, all the surgeons met to discuss their procedures. There was a lot of information sharing, ideas on improving procedures, and suggestions on how to serve their patients better. Bagley had always found these meetings beneficial because many new mechanical devices, medicines, and methods improved the quality of care and speed of recovery. Penn Medicine's large clinical department was constantly involved in new clinical trials. Simply put, you never know when a vital breakthrough is approaching.

It was a typical day for Bagley until about 4 p.m. On his way to his office, he stopped to get a cup of coffee to finalize some charts. As he left with his coffee, a good-sized man came behind him. The guy stepped in front of Bagley and blocked his way. The man said, "You Stephen Bagley?"

"Dr. Bagley, but yes, I am. Who are you?"

"It doesn't matter who I am, just that I need to talk to you for a minute. You are the guy who did the surgery for Franklin Johns, aren't you?"

Bagley said, "That's confidential and privileged between doctors and patients. I can't talk to you about patients, either mine or my colleagues." Bagley stepped to the side and started to move.

Edwards took Bagley by the arm and said, "Then I am going to assume you are the surgeon involved with Johns. I suggest you find a way to keep Johns off the field for the rest of the season. It would be in your best interest to do so."

Bagley pulled his arm from Edwards' grasp and said, "Who do you think you are? Are you threatening me?"

"That is exactly what I am doing. And I think you should take this advice very seriously. In fact, I misspoke earlier when I said suggest; I meant to say demand. You will make sure that Johns stays out of action for the duration. Talk to the Eagle doctors, talk to anybody you want to, but I expect that Franklin Johns is done for the year. Do and say whatever you want."

Bagley was getting nervous, but he didn't want to back down. He said, "And what if I don't do that?"

Edwards looked closely at Bagley's face and said, "You don't want to go down that road. It won't end pleasantly for you; you can be sure of that." Edwards patted Bagley on the shoulder, had a smirk on his face, turned, and started to walk away.

Bagley was shocked, but he had at least enough mental control to want to get a picture of the guy, so he covertly used his phone camera to snap a pic. He wasn't sure what he was going to do with it, but for some reason, he thought it was a good idea.

After Edwards left the building, Bagley stood in the same spot thinking about his four years of undergrad schooling, where he needed to get all A's. He remembered his four years of medical school. He recalled his three years of residency and a year of a fellowship. And he reflected on being an orthopedic surgeon at Penn for almost 12 years.

This was the first time he had ever been afraid!

Chapter Seventeen

Sharon was up early because she was going to have a busy day. She needed to meet with both the CSI team and the ME. She wasn't too optimistic about what she would get regarding clues and hints, but she had to go through the process anyway.

I wanted to sleep in again, but I got up early, even for me. I wanted to send the Linc data to Linda at IC3 in DC. I was right that I would need a few more computer sticks. By the time I had put all the data together, it was a total of nine sticks. Lots of info, but I was sure Linda could quickly process it.

I had initially planned to FedEx the sticks to Linda, but I didn't have a class today, so I decided to call Linda to check on her availability. I called her, and when she picked up the phone, she said, "IC3, Linda Willis."

"Linda, this is Ben Stone."

"Ben, nice to hear from you. How are the data going for our project?"

"I put together nine computer sticks. It's even more than I thought it would be."

She said, "That's a bit, but we have processors that can quickly handle that amount. You going to have it couriered down to my office?"

"Actually, since I don't have class today, I was thinking about taking the train down to DC, and we could have a bite to eat. I've checked the schedule for Amtrak, and I think I could get to your office by about 2 p.m. My treat if you have time and interest."

"Ben, that is very nice of you. I have some time this afternoon, and around 2 p.m. would be fine. I would love to meet you in person so you can tell me about some of your adventures that Emily has hinted at. Much more exciting than grinding out numbers as we do at IC3."

"Sharon and I have had some interesting events, but remember that I'm an accounting professor. Much of my time is spent teaching, grading papers, and writing recommendation letters. Our adventures are the exception, not the rule. Or at least for me. Sharon does have a pretty crazy life as a homicide detective."

Linda chuckled and said, "I'm sure that's true. Anyway, I'm guessing you know the building we're in. Just have me paged when you get to the front desk, and I'll come down to let you in."

"Sounds great. See you In a few hours."

After I hung up with Linda, I called Sharon. She often can't pick up, so I leave a message. However, this time she picked up on the first ring. "Well, Dr. Stone. What brings you into my world today? Gotta decide on what's for dinner?"

"That's always an important decision for us, but I wanted to tell you I am taking a train ride down to DC to meet with Linda from IC3. I decided to meet her in person since I am asking for a lot of assistance, and meeting in person seemed appropriate. Is that okay?"

"Sure, that's fine. As you know, I have a couple of meetings today, so I will likely be a little late. When do you think you might be home?"

"Probably around 6. By the way, how's your day going?"

"Meeting with the CSI team at noon and then the ME around 3. I've already talked to each, and there may not have much to say, but both had a couple of ideas to discuss. And just like you're going to DC, sometimes meeting in person is best. Good luck with your meeting."

"Same to you. I'll call you when I'm on the train coming back. We'll debrief tonight. Love you."

"Love you, too."

It was still fun to hear Sharon say that, even though we have been saying "I love you" for a while now. Since it took a while for us to say it to each other, it still hasn't completely sunk in for me. I never asked Sharon how she felt about saying it. Maybe I should ask her sometime. Or perhaps I should leave it alone! Probably a better idea!

While I was getting all the sticks together, Sharon decided to write out everything she had on this case. Sometimes she needs to see everything in writing to get a handle on it. As always, she hoped pondering all the variables might lead to a breakthrough. Of course, sometimes she just kills some trees.

The first thing she did was lay out all she had on the murder—which happened around 10 p.m. at the Rhawnhurst Bar and Grill. Linebacker for the Giants named Meadows. Two guys likely jumped the linebacker. Both guys appeared to have knives. One of them stabbed Meadows in the back. The knife went in deep, so it must have been a good-sized knife. Guy came out of the bar for a smoke, saw Meadows on the ground, and could see the blood. The guy yells, and the two fellas with knives take off. The witness doesn't see much other than their general build and size. He uses his phone to dial 911 and then opens the door to yell for help. Asks if anyone has any medical training. No one does, but one of the bartenders brought cloths to help with the bleeding. The paramedics arrived, checked for vitals, saw Meadows had already lost a lot of blood, and rushed him to Penn's ER. Meadows was pronounced dead on arrival.

As Sharon thought through what she had, the obvious question was why these guys came prepared with knives. The knife wound appeared much too big for a knife someone would carry around. So that told Sharon that this meeting was planned, not just a couple of guys who got drunk and pulled a knife. But then the question became: Why did Meadows meet with these two? They didn't just happen to show up together. Sharon had checked and found that Meadows lived in North Jersey. Not likely; he came all the way to Rhawnhurst because of its great food and beer. So, what brought him down there?

Sharon got a call from the switchboard as she sat at her desk trying to assemble some ideas. She said, "Levin."

"Sharon, it's Larry Perkins from CSI. I know you are coming to our lab soon, but I just got an interesting call. Another Giants football player named Fred Harris, a safety, not that matters, just called our desk. He apparently has some important information about the guy who stabbed Meadows."

Sharon said, "What's he got to say?"

"Harris says that he knows that Meadows took a bribe to hit Franklin Johns in the knee and put him out of a game. He says that some gamblers paid Meadows to the tune of 50 large."

Sharon said, "Larry, given I've got almost nothing, that is great news. Can this guy Harris come down and talk to us?"

"Actually, he can't. The Giants have an away game at the Bears this week, and they need to leave to make their flight. But he said he is happy to Facetime with you in about an hour. He gave me his phone number. Would that work for you?"

"Larry, that will work great for me. Finally, I might have caught a little break with this case. Thanks for letting me know."

Sharon put down her phone, sat back, and thought: Progress, not perfection. But at least there was some progress!

Chapter Eighteen

Sharon decided to continue going through her research on the murder. It really wasn't that much right now, but she had time to kill until she heard from the Harris.

As she went through what she had so far, it became clear that she would have expanded the link between Johns and the gamblers. She didn't know how she would do it, but she had to find out some names of the gamblers. It was vital because the gamblers were crucial to unlocking what happened.

As she was shaking her head, suddenly her phone rang with a Facetime call. She took the call, saw a picture of a huge guy, and said, "Detective Levin."

"Detective, my name is Fred Harris. I play for the Giants, and I'm contacting you about Len Meadows. Sorry I couldn't meet with you, but we're at the airport waiting to fly out for our game with Chicago."

"No problem. Thanks for taking the time to tell me what happened. So, what did happen?"

He replied, "Well, it's pretty straightforward. Len and I were good friends, and he took me to lunch one day to tell me that he had taken a bribe to help the Philadelphia Eagles lose the game last week. Some mobsters gave Len 50 grand to make sure that the Eagles' top running back, Franklin Johns, was put out of the game. Len felt a little guilty about what he did, so he decided to talk to someone and picked me."

Sharon replied, "So I understand that part. I need to know if you know who the guys paid the bribe are."

"Len never gave me any names. He just said he had some financial problems, so he decided to take the bribe when offered. As you may or may not know, football players take injuries very seriously. Practically every player could be put out of a game, so while we are aggressive about tackling opponents, you're not supposed to put anyone out of the game, at least not intentionally. Just isn't done."

"Any ideas about what happened to Meadows?"

"I've given it a lot of thought, and about all I can come up with is that somehow the gamblers found out about Len meeting with me. I mentioned what happened to some teammates, but none would be talking to the gamblers. So, I don't know how they found out."

"Well, all I can tell you is that I have been a cop for a lot of years, and it is astounding how much chatter can get around. If I had to guess, the gamblers caught wind of the bribe and decided to ensure Meadows didn't spread the info to law enforcement. But how did the gamblers get Meadows down to Philly if that's the case?"

Harris replied, "All I know is that I suggested that Len donate some of the money to a football charity. I told him what he did was wrong and that maybe donating some of his dough would make up for what he did wrong. I told him if he wanted to make amends for injuring Johns, he needed to donate a substantial sum. Dropping a grand didn't matter much. If he had taken my advice, maybe it turned out that he needed the donation money back. But, as I said, I'm just guessing."

"That might be how it went down. I know a few local gamblers who owe me a favor or two, so I will make the rounds. I appreciate your help. Have a good game!"

"Thanks! Chicago has a decent season, but we've been playing pretty well lately. I like our chances. Good luck with your job."

Sharon closed her phone and sat for just a minute. She wasn't sure her chat with Frank did that much good, but it did give her an idea about asking around the local gambling world. Somebody surely knows something about how the murder of Meadows went down. She just had to find the right person. She knew that most gamblers constantly change phone numbers, so rattling phones probably wouldn't help much. She figured she would have to go old school and spend most of the day knocking on many doors.

It wasn't fun, but Sharon knew from experience that sometimes the low-tech way is best.

Meanwhile, I had made it down to DC. I made it up to Linda's building and asked the receptionist to call Linda. A few minutes later, a tall thin woman came out of the elevator.

I walked over and said, "Linda?"

She smiled and replied, "Dr. Ben Stone, I presume. Thanks so much for coming down." We shook hands.

I said, "Happy to come down. You're helping me out with this Aramark project. Anyway, got any suggestions on where to have a late lunch?"

"If you like Chinese, there is a great place two blocks down the street. It only has chicken but has a lot of choices. The sides are great. Sound good?"

"Lead the way."

Linda and I started our short walk to the Chinese restaurant. While we walked, she asked me about my trip, and I asked her about her day. We chatted until we got to the restaurant.

We arrived at a restaurant named Little Chicken. The place was pretty crowded, but they had room for two over on the side and took us straight to a table.

We sat, and the waiter left us menus. I glanced at the menu and asked, "So, got anything you recommend?"

"Their chicken salad sandwich is fantastic. A side of coleslaw rounds it out. They have alcohol, but I don't drink at work. Please feel free to have a cocktail if you like."

"Food sounds good, but I'll pass on the drink. I'm not much of a drinker, so I have to pace myself. Iced tea will work for me."

The waiter returned, and Linda asked for two of the same food choices. She decided on a Diet Coke to drink.

After the waiter left, Linda said, "So, Ben, I assume you have all the computer sticks I'm going to need to get this started."

I reached into my briefcase and took out a small box. I handed it to Linda and said, "Nine sticks as promised."

She took the box and set it aside. "I'll get it all forwarded to one of our tech guys I like. I'm pretty sure he can get started soon."

"That's great. As I said, I appreciate your assistance."

"Ben, we're part of the FBI. It's our job. Anyway, I wanted to talk with you about all the adventures you and Sharon have had. After you contacted me, I did a Google search, and you two have been in crazy situations."

I laughed and said, "Linda, some people think we're making this all up. Sometimes I can't believe all the nutty things we've been involved in. Got a particular favorite you've heard about?"

"All the international stuff is interesting, but I haven't been to any of those countries. BUT I love New Orleans. I have been there four times, including Mardi Gras once. Vampires. You found vampires down in New Orleans."

I laughed again and said, "Not exactly vampires. People who thought they were vampires. People who acted like vampires. But people who killed some folks to make it look like vampires were the killers."

"That is so cool!"

"It wasn't that cool because they killed three people."

"Yes, that is true, but the story was really interesting. Sorry that people got killed, but it's a fascinating read."

Our food arrived, and Linda and I started to eat. I told her that the food was excellent. She asked me some more questions, including about the Outer Banks. It was clear that Linda thought Sharon and I had a much more exciting life than she did. She didn't entirely appreciate that we had been in some truly scary, perhaps deadly, situations. She just thought that we only had fun.

Our lunch was excellent, and we talked about her job and a few things about her life. I picked up the tab, and we went back to her office. I thanked her again, and she said she would contact me once she had some results. We shook hands, and I headed to Union Station to return to Philly.

I decided that making the extra effort to meet Linda was worth it. I felt confident that she would help me with this project.

What I didn't know, and neither did Sharon, was that just grinding out numbers and statistics would qualify as fun when the next phase of this adventure began!

Chapter Nineteen

Bagley didn't sleep at all last night. However, he had been through many sleepless nights between med school, residency, and a fellowship. It was just one of the things he needed to learn and accept. However, last night he was awake for a much more fearful reason.

After the guy who threatened him left, Bagley called security at the hospital and the Philadelphia police. The cops came and took his statement. However, he didn't have that much to tell them. He gave them a copy of the picture he took, and they said they would forward everything to the investigative arm of the police. If they found out anything, they would let him know about it.

However, one of the cops had heard about Sharon's case involving Franklin Johns. He decided to tell Bagley about it in case he heard anything helpful. He even gave Bagley Sharon's phone number at the station to provide Bagley with a bit of comfort.

Bagley decided to call out sick that day. He had no surgeries planned, so he moved his appointments to another day. None of the appointments that day were that urgent, and Bagley felt he needed to take more action other than what he had done so far.

Bagley decided to reach out to Sharon. He called her number, and she picked up on the first ring. "Detective Levin."

"Detective, my name is Dr. Stephen Bagley down at Penn."

Sharon replied, "Good morning, Doctor. I just got a message about what happened yesterday afternoon. Sorry to hear about that. I was going to contact you later today, so I'm glad you called me."

Bagley said, "Well, Detective, I've never had anything like that has ever happened to me. I'm a bit frightened, but I am also furious.

I can't believe a guy just walked up to me at the hospital and threatened me. I contacted you to see if you can do anything to help me with this situation."

"I'm a homicide cop, so normally I wouldn't be the head honcho on your problem, but because there is a link between my case and your issue, I'll have your case transferred to me. Do you recall anything you didn't include in your statement yesterday?"

"I don't think so. Unsurprisingly, I was up all night but couldn't think of anything to add. However, I would appreciate it if you and I could meet and discuss the next steps. Just sitting and waiting is not my style."

"Can't say I'm surprised," said Sharon. "Know a few docs personally, and they are doers, not sitters. Are you working at the hospital today?"

"Actually, no. I took the day off. First time in a long, long time that I took a day off. Guess that indicates that this whole thing slightly rattles me."

Sharon said, "I've got a few things to take care of right now, but could you come into the stationhouse this afternoon? Say 2 p.m.? You and I can discuss at length what steps we might take. And by the way, being a little rattled by what happened is normal and expected."

"2 p.m. works for me. Where should we meet?"

"I'm down at the station in Northeast Philly off the Boulevard. Where do you live?" asked Sharon.

"I'm over in Villanova. But I am happy to drive to the Northeast to meet you. It probably will take about an hour, but that's not a problem."

"That's helpful because, as I said, my dance card is pretty full today. What's your email? I will send you the specific address to the station." Bagley gave her his email, and she then quickly sent him the location.

Bagley said, "I appreciate your help."

"It's my job. See you in a few hours." With that, they hung up.

The problem was, what was Bagley to do until 2 p.m.? He knew he probably couldn't sleep, so how could he occupy the time? He decided that one thing he could do was to Google a few ideas on how to protect himself if necessary.

He already knew a kick to the balls would put a guy down. The question was: What if your attacker moves to the side to protect his jewels? Bagley pulled up a couple of videos that showed him how to jab toward the throat, slam to the chest, and grab the attacker to one side. They all looked like something he could handle, but a kick to the balls was probably the best choice. Bagley knew that he didn't have to have a medical degree to go for the nuts. But he did know that he needed to have the courage to kick the assailant.

Bagley knew a lot about the human body, and he was confident that he could knee someone if required and all those years of medical training made it pretty easy for Bagley to envision how this might go down. It made him feel a little more confident. But even with that renewed confidence, Bagley decided to leave in time to pick up some pepper spray. It never hurts to have a backup plan.

Bagley wasn't hungry, and he was living on caffeine right now. He occupied his mind by reviewing some of the medical journals he regularly received. He knew he wasn't focused on what was before him, but it was worth a try.

At about 12:30, he decided to head out. He got an Uber ride to the station. He knew he might get to the station a little early, but he also knew there were coffee shops and delis where he could hang out if need be.

He got to the station at 1:30 and found a Starbucks where he could sit. Again, he tried to look at some research journals, but it was a waste of time. Too many things are bouncing around in his head.

At 1:55, he entered the station house and asked for Sharon. The sergeant in charge called Sharon's phone, and Sharon told the sergeant to tell Bagley she would be out in just a few minutes.

Sharon came out and recognized that Bagley was sitting at the chair for guests. She said, "Dr. Bagley, correct?"

Bagley stood and said, "I am. Thanks for taking the time to talk to me."

"Not a problem. As I said, it's my job."

They went back to Sharon's office. She offered coffee or tea. Bagley declined. Sharon said, "Scotch?"

"Not much of a drinker, but the temptation for a cocktail is high right now."

Sharon smiled, "I'm sure that's the case. So have you remembered anything from what happened that wasn't in your police report?"

"Again, not really. I tried to be very thorough when I spoke to the police earlier. I wanted to ask you if you think I am in any danger, and if so, what should I do?"

Sharon replied, "Hard for me to tell at this point. We just got a copy of the picture you took, and we are running it through facial recognition, but we haven't had a match come up yet. But I'm still optimistic that we'll get a hit. Sometimes it takes a little time."

At that point, Sharon got a text from CSI that she should look at her email. She told Bagley to hang on for a minute and pulled up the email. Facial rec didn't show anyone on the FBI files. Sharon knew that such a finding probably meant this guy had not been arrested, or at least for a long time, so his face was not on the FBI files.

Sharon said, "Well, I'm sorry to tell you, but the facial recognition didn't come back with a match. Our Crime Scene Investigation can use a couple of other databases, but I have to admit that they will not likely get a hit."

Bagley said, "All I know about CSI is what I've watched on a few crime shows. Anyway, what do you think I should do?"

"Well, I could provide police security, but I can probably only offer it for a few days. Not likely that my chief can authorize very much. You can hire personal security yourself, but I don't know how long you would want to do that. We have some ideas about tracking the perpetrators, but we don't have many solid ideas. It could take a while. I would suggest using Uber or Lyft to get back and forth to the hospital. I doubt the guy you saw will try to jump you in the hospital. Penn has excellent security. I assume you have good security at your home."

Bagley nodded and said, "Excellent security at my house. I assume you are going to give Mr. Johns some extra security?"

"The Eagles are paying for round-the-clock security for his home and his trips to the rehab center."

"So, I guess I will just be aware of my surroundings and be careful," said Bagley.

Sharon said, "I wish I could be more definitive, but I promise to keep in touch with you with any new findings. In short, I'll keep you in the loop."

"Detective, that's all I can ask for right now. I appreciate your time." Bagley put out his hand.

Sharon took his hand and shook it. She said, "Don't worry, we'll get this bastard."

For the first time, Bagley actually felt somewhat at ease. He didn't know that Sharon and I were the ones who would be in danger quite soon!

Chapter Twenty

The following day, I was up early. I had a 10 a.m. class, so I needed to leave for Temple at about 9:15 am. It's an intermediate accounting class, so I didn't need to prep. Done it many, many times.

Once I got to Temple, I had a few minutes to drop off my backpack at my office. Just as I was heading out to the class, my phone rang. I decided to answer it because some strange things were happening these days, and I wanted to ensure Sharon was okay.

"Dr. Stone."

"Hi, Ben; it's Linda Willis at IC3."

"Nice to hear from you. However, you can't already have an analysis from the Aramark case. It was just yesterday that I dropped off the sticks."

Linda chuckled and said, "I told you we have a lot of computing power we can use to crunch out data. I'm not done, but I have some initial findings that I think you will find interesting. Got some time to talk?"

"Actually, I have class in five minutes, but I'll be done about noon. Can I call you then?"

"I'll be in my office, so sure that works. Have a good class."

As I walked to class, I thought getting Linda and IC3 involved was an excellent idea. Of course, since I didn't know what she had so far, I couldn't say how much it would not help.

The class went fine. I returned the last exam I had done, and overall, the results were pretty good. The average grade was 88, much higher than that class's norm. When I had determined the overall average, I thought that somehow the students had figured out some way to cheat. But since I wrote the exam from scratch, I couldn't determine whether Course Hero or any other website could make a difference. I chalked it up to excellent teaching!

I returned to my office and called Linda. She picked up on the first ring and said, "Linda Willis at IC3."

"Linda, it's Ben Stone."

"How did your class go, Ben?"

"They did very well. Intermediate accounting and an average of 88. Sometimes when the grades are that high, I figure at first, somehow, they found a way to cheat."

Linda laughed, saying, "Sorry to say, Ben, but you sound a little cantankerous. Could be you're just a great instructor."

"Sometimes, I try that trick on myself. Occasionally it works, and it did today. I wrote the exam out myself, so there is no way anyone could have had any insider information. But I've been in this academic world for a while and have seen some creative ways students have cheated. Can't help but wonder when the grades are higher than expected."

"I can certainly understand your concern. With my job, it is amazing how much technology has changed how people can cheat others out of money, which brings me to my initial findings. You ready to hear about it?"

"Hanging on every word," said I.

"So, I confirmed your findings about the Benford analysis. It is obvious that the accounts payable down at the Linc have been manipulated. But more than that, we found that to have manipulated the AP work, it had to be by someone inside the Linc. Maybe you already thought that, but based on our analysis, it's got to be the accounting manager down at the Linc. What's the guy's name?"

I replied, "A fellow named Maury Johnson. And you're right; I figured he had something to do with it, but I wasn't quite clear how he pulled it off. Any suggestions?"

"The most common accounts payable fraud schemes are billing schemes, check fraud, automated clearing house fraud, expense reports, kickback schemes, and conflict of interest schemes.

Billing fraud is number one, and we see it all the time. The criminal sets up a lot of fictitious billing invoices, they get paid, and the money goes into the criminal's account. It's the simplest fraud to commit. But we can now track the fictitious accounts and determine where the money has been routed. And we found out the routing source with your case."

"That sounds great! How does it work?"

Linda responded, "It appears that the good Mr. Johnson has over 30 fake accounts under fictitious names. All he does is move the money to the fake account and then to his own accounts. The trick is that his fake accounts appear appropriate, which is why the internal auditors at Aramark and the external ones at Deloitte didn't find them. I can forward the names of the fake accounts to you today."

I said, "I can't believe you found all this so quickly. Thank you so much for your help."

Linda replied, "Glad to help out. I hope you can gather enough evidence to take this guy down. It pisses me off when people who are supposed to be professional accountants who should protect other people's money instead steal it from them."

"Don't worry. Once I get a little more evidence, I'll get Sharon involved. She'll figure out a way to nab this guy. She's a homicide detective, so most of what she deals with are murders, but people who steal other people's money drive her nuts. Sharon knows many working-class people who work hard at their jobs to provide for their families. People who cheat piss her off."

"Well, I wish you the best of luck. Let me know if you need any more assistance." With that, she hung up.

I sat back and thought for a few minutes. While Linda didn't uncover any blockbuster findings, she confirmed what I had found out. Now I just needed to figure out how to confront Maury Johnson and get him to trip up by saying the wrong thing.

Maybe I could get Sharon to have a "chat" with him. When she does that, she usually gets some results.

Chapter Twenty-One

Frank Welborn had just gotten off the phone, and he was pissed. He slammed his cell phone down and cursed out loud. Edwards wasn't around, but Forman was. He asked Welborn, "What the hell is wrong with you?"

Welborn replied loudly, "I just got a tip from a guy I know connected to the cops. It has to do with that Philly homicide cop we heard about. Apparently, she has spent a lot of time looking into our business. I'm not sure how much she found out, but she is devoting a lot of effort tracking down Bruno and Bennie. I don't think she has their names yet, but she's getting close. And if that wasn't enough, I know from the orderly at Penn Hospital that the doc there met with this cop to talk about when Edwards threatened the doc. A lot of shit is going down right now, and I don't like where it's heading. We need to take action!"

Forman said, "And what do you think we should do? It sounds like the cops are all over us right now. We can't let anything out about what we had to do with the football player who got killed or Franklin Johns. We have to keep a very low profile right now."

Welborn replied, "We can't just do that right now. We've taken a very sizable hit on our bets of late and are way behind what we need to cover. And we dropped 50 large for the dumbass who got killed even though that helped us make a lot on the Eagles-Giants game."

At that moment, Edwards walked into the office. He said, "How's it going, guys? Have a good day?"

Welborn said, "No, we are not having a good day. We are having a very shitty day. I told Forman that the Philly cop we heard was snooping around has been finding out some information about what was happened. She's talked to that Giants player who knew about Meadows and the bribe we gave him to knock Johns out of the Giants game. She also spoke to the doc you threatened. This doc will have security around the clock and won't tell the Eagles that Johns can't play. If Johns does recover from his injury, he might be able to play before the end of the season. That might seriously affect whether we will make the big score we need with the Giants game up at MetLife Stadium. That a big issue we need to fix."

Forman said, "But even if Johns gets back on the field, do you think he will be at 100%? It could be he makes an appearance. In fact, having him on the field could be to our advantage. He could have a big negative effect on the game."

Welborn said, "From what I hear from the orderly, Johns could likely be 100%. More importantly, the team really likes him, and they may rise even higher on the competition scale. In short, they may try even harder with him in the game."

Edwards slammed his hand on the table and said, "Okay, that is bad news. But we've got to do something."

Welborn said, "I agree, but John Boy thinks we should just sit tight."

"All I'm saying is that I don't see a way out of this right now," suggested Forman. "We've got cops looking into our affairs, and laying low might be best. Does one of you have a better idea that we should use?"

"We need someone to have a serious discussion with this cop," said Edwards. "We need her to back off right now."

"So, you think we need to take on a Philly cop?" said Forman. "Are you fucking insane? Some of the cops in the city may not be great, but many are. Also, if we try to threaten a cop, all the other cops will come after us. They take care of their own."

Both Welborn and Edwards both thought for a minute. Then Welborn smiled and said, "We go after her accounting professor boyfriend. He's only a fucking accounting professor. How tough can he be? We scare the shit out of him, and she'll leave us alone."

Edwards said, "Now, that is a good idea. We make sure the professor is scared to death. Like you said, how hard can that be? And it might not stop the lady cop completely, but she will be distracted while we finish our gambling business to end the season. As we said, after the football season ends, all three of us should take a trip to the islands for a couple of months until things completely calm down."

Forman asked, "And how exactly will we know that the lady cop isn't around? If we have someone go after the prof and she's around, that could end badly for us."

Edwards replied, "We get someone, maybe Bruno and Bennie, to find out where this guy lives. Then we have him threatened. We have them do it during the day. The lady cop has to be at work. The prof will be alone when we make our move."

Welborn smiled and said, "It's a good idea, but you're right that we shouldn't personally do it. We need a dumbass or two to take care of this. Bruno and Bennie are good choices. Any of you talked to Bruno or Bennie lately?"

Forman replied, "I'm still not convinced this is a good idea, but I know how to contact Bruno and Bennie. They haven't been picking up their phone, probably ditched it, but I know a bar they hang out in South Philly. I can leave a message that one of them should call us. I know they hit this bar a lot, and I'll give the bartender a nice tip to get the message to one of them."

"I'll admit that this may not be the best plan we have ever had," said Edwards, "But we can't just do nothing and hope that things work out. We've gotta take some action, and I vote for reasonable action versus no action."

Welborn said, "I agree. Get in touch with Bruno or Bennie, and we'll figure out a way to put the fear of God into this professor. Like I said, how hard could it be?"

Little did they know!

Chapter Twenty-Two

I decided to work from home today. I didn't have class or office hours, and I wanted to make some progress on the Aramark and Linc project. Linda from IC3 had been accommodating, but I still had some things I needed to do.

Sharon gave me a call as I was powering through all the data. I picked it up and said, "Hello, this is Ben Stone, the best-looking accounting professor in the country."

"That would be more impressive if there were good-looking accounting professors in general, but there are not. The bar is not that high!"

I laughed and said, "Wow, that stings. You do make me feel all warm and fuzzy. Anyway, what's going on?"

"I was thinking about running to the house for a quick lunch. I've got to run around downtown on another case, so I'd be in the area," said Sharon.

"Works for me. Do you want me to order something, or will you pick something up?"

"I'll surprise you!"

"Uh oh, that doesn't always work out for me, but I'm willing to take a chance. See you soon."

I knew the next thing I needed to do was examine all the fictional accounts Linda forwarded me. It was quite a number, but there were hundreds of real accounts, so I was glad that Linda helped me figure out the fake ones. At first, I thought I would relay all the information to Aramark and let them take over. But I decided to do more digging to try to be as comprehensive as possible with what I gave them.

I had spent over an hour combing through all the documents as I tried to figure out how best to attack the problem, and then my door rang. Since some of my cases have included some unsavory characters of late, I had had a peephole installed in my front door. I looked through it and didn't see anyone. Since I couldn't see anyone, I decided not to answer. After a couple of minutes, the door rang again. I looked at the peephole once more, and no one was visible. I started to get a little nervous. I considered calling 911, but I was still hoping whomever it was would leave.

Then there was a knock at the door. It was a booming knock. A guy yelled through the door, "Hi, I'm selling Girl Scout cookies. Can you open the door?"

I said, "Thanks, but I don't want any."

The voice said, "But it helps little girls make some money. Plus, the cookies are really, really good."

"Like I said, not interested. Sorry."

Then I heard someone slam at my door. Now I was concerned. I started to call 911, but then I decided to try Sharon. I called her, and she said, "Hey, I'm on my way. Just around the corner. Got a food surprise."

I quietly said, "Someone is trying to break into the house. They're banging on the door."

"Keep the door locked. I'm less than five minutes out. I'll contact 911 for backup."

"Okay."

At that moment, a voice came loudly through the door. "Okay, since you are not going for the cookies scam, let me tell you something. We will find you even if we can't get into your house right now. And when we do, it will not be good. We want your girlfriend cop to stop snooping around about the football player who got killed. And we are expecting you to stay out of the Franklin Johns' business. Have her stay away from him, too."

I knew Sharon was nearby, so I replied, "And what happens if she doesn't?"

The voice said, "You're a fucking professor. You aren't tough, so you won't like what happens when we find you."

I heard Sharon's voice right then, and she said, "Gentlemen, put your hands up in the air. Don't try anything stupid; my gun is aimed at your heads. And backup is coming from right around the corner."

I could take a full breath for the first time in a few minutes. Sharon said, "Ben, you can open the door. I'm here, and also backup has arrived."

I unlocked the door and saw that Sharon had two guys handcuffed by uniformed cops. Sharon had put her gun back into her holster. She approached me and said, "You have the most interesting things happen for an accounting professor." With that, she   hugged   me.

I smiled and said, "Glad you decided to come home for lunch. By the way, why does this stuff keep happening to me?"

"Just lucky, I guess. The uniforms are going to take these two idiots into the station. I'm going to find out what the hell is going on. But first, we're still going to have lunch. Found a Jamaican place on the way home."

"As long as it includes some alcohol, whatever you want is fine."

"Little early for a cocktail, isn't it?" said Sharon.

"I think I can make an exception today."

Sharon smiled, "I think I can, too. Beer or wine?"

"Whiskey. It's been a tough day already!"

She smiled and got me a shot to have with our lunch. We decided not to talk about what had happened right now. She knew she would have more information later, so we decided to discuss how the upcoming Eagles games were crucial. We didn't know much or even care much about the Eagles, but Sharon tried to distract me for about an hour. Then she told me she needed to head into the precinct and debrief the two guys she had just caught. Naturally, she told me to keep the door locked and call if anything else happened. You didn't have to ask me twice.

When Sharon arrived at the precinct, she saw that the guys she had arrested were in separate cells in the holding area. The cops on duty said neither of the guys said anything. They didn't even ask for a lawyer, which is somewhat weird. People who get busted almost always scream for a lawyer. Seen it too many times on TV, but these two didn't seem interested in it.

Sharon discovered their names, **Bruno Lord and Bennie Wilson**, and they were just some cheap muscle. She spoke to both individually, and neither had anything to say. Sharon figured both had been behind bars at some point and maybe spending a few days locked up would get them to talk. She would find out as much as she could about them, but she could tell they weren't running the show.

But that was her next step. Bruno and Bennie were going to be in jail for a while. Right now, she needed to talk to a pro football player!

Chapter Twenty-Three

Franklin Johns lived in a lovely home out near Ardmore. It was not a mansion because Franklin knew that being a pro running back usually meant you might get five years before you go down because of an injury. He wanted to make sure he provided for his family and himself.

He had set up his house to include room for his father, mother, and younger brother. He had grown up very poor in Goldsboro, North Carolina, but he ensured his family was provided for once he made it big. He also made substantial donations to Goldsboro itself. Even though his life in Goldsboro was rough, he needed to give back to his hometown.

Franklin was sitting in his living room watching game films. Even though it was all he could do while going through rehab, he wanted to be ready to go when the doctors gave him the green light to get back on the field. While he was watching, the doorbell rang. Franklin always had two security guards, so one of them, Rusty Brown, went to answer the door. The second one, a woman named Laura Booth, stood behind Brown in case something happened.

Brown opened the door and said, "How can I help you?"

Sharon replied, "I'm Detective Sharon Levin. I'd like to speak to Mr. Johns."

"Can I see your badge?"

Sharon pulled out her badge and handed it to Brown. Brown looked closely at the badge and then nodded. "Please come in," he said.

Sharon entered the house and saw that Johns was sitting near his TV. She said, "Mr. Johns, I'm Detective Sharon Levin from the Philadelphia police. I want to talk to you about some things."

Johns turned off the TV and said, "Please call me Franklin. Have a seat. What can I do for you?"

Sharon said, "And I'm Sharon. I wanted to discuss your security arrangements."

"Well, as you can see, I have two guards who rotate around the clock. I feel like I'm pretty safe right now."

Sharon said, "That's quite true. It looks like you've got some solid security for you and your family. But I wanted to discuss with you if any other family members, friends, or even any other Eagles' players could pressure you not to play."

"The people in this house make up my family. I have a few uncles, a nephew, and a cousin or two in North Carolina, but I doubt anyone would know about them. I stay in touch but question if anyone outside my family knows about them. I have many friends and, of course, my teammates, but again, it's unlikely that someone would want to try to leverage them to get to me. Anyone who follows the Eagles knows who our players are, but again, I doubt whoever these scumbags are in this whole thing would try to target another player. Plus, we have over 45 players, so I don't think you could provide security for all of them."

Sharon was a bit surprised. Franklin Johns was more thoughtful and much more courteous than she thought a pro football player would be. She was impressed. She said, "Well, what about your backup at running back, Billy Sans? I heard you may be back before the end of the season, but Mr. Sans will be filling in for you for at least three weeks. If he goes down, the Eagles would be in big trouble."

Johns smiled and replied, "Funny you should ask. I heard just yesterday that the Eagles are now providing security for Billy. I guess great minds think alike."

Sharon smiled back and said, "It does seem like the Eagles have covered all the bases. I'm very impressed."

"Don't be impressed by me; I didn't do anything other than get injured. It's the Eagles who have taken care of everything. I try to work hard at my rehab, so I might really get back before the season ends."

"I wish you the best of luck getting back on the field. I must admit that I'm not a huge football fan, but I hope you get back soon. Plus, naturally, I hope that you and your family remain safe."

Johns said, "I appreciate all you and the rest of Philly's finest have done for me. In fact, and you probably don't know, I studied accounting during college. I want to meet sometime with your friend, Dr. Stone, and talk about how I might be able to use my accounting degree when I leave football."

Sharon had an astonished look. Johns smiled and said, "Yeah, I know. Everyone assumes that a football player at a big-time school majored in recreational studies or something like that. And there are a number of those types, to be sure. But I listened to my college coach, who encouraged me to get a real degree in a real subject. All the practice, travel, and games take up much time, but our coach wanted us to have more than just football. I didn't graduate with honors, but I did okay. About a 3.1 average is better than some of the non-football accounting students did."

Sharon smiled again and said, "Very impressive, Franklin. I never went to college."

"Yeah, but you get to save some lives. That's a bigger deal than rushing for over 100 yards in a game."

"Not according to an Eagles fan. But I appreciate what you said. Anyway, it sounds like you have your security pretty well in hand, so there is not much that I can add. All I can say again is good luck."

Johns said, "Thanks a lot. By the way, I would suggest discussing the overall security at the Linc. In fact, maybe you should talk with our manager and coach. They certainly know much more about that thing than I do. I could get you set up with a meeting."

"That's a great idea. And to be honest, Ben, overwise known at Dr. Stone, has a case involving someone who appears to be stealing money from the Linc concessions. Maybe we could kill two birds."

"Happy to help in any way I can," said Johns. "I'll ensure the coach and manager get you some premier tickets. Maybe we can turn you into football fans."

Sharon smiled and said, "You never know, do you?"

Chapter Twenty-Four

The gamblers, Welborn, Forman, and Edwards, were all three very pissed off. They had trusted Bruno and Bennie would be able to scare the accounting professor's homicide girlfriend into shutting up. But the timing was terrible for when she showed up. Now all three had to be concerned about Bruno and Bennie staying quiet.

Welborn said, "I can't believe this homicide bitch showed up just when Bruno and Bennie were at the professor's house. What are the fucking odds?"

Forman replied, "It sure sucks, but it happened, and we need to do something about it. Any suggestions?"

Welborn said, "I've worked with Bruno and Bennie before, and I sort of trust them to keep their mouths shut, at least for now."

Edwards said, "Yeah, but are they going to stay quiet when the cops start to put together some things about the football player they killed?"

Welborn replied, "I don't think the cops have any serious evidence right now about Meadows. It's all circumstantial. The cops don't have any hard proof connecting the football player who got killed and us. In fact, I don't think the cops really have anything on Bruno and Bennie other than threatening the professor. I'm sure this lady cop will pressure Bruno and Bennie, but they've been down that road before. As I said, I think they can stay quiet for now. But maybe we should get someone to message Bruno and Bennie about keeping their mouths shut."

Forman said, "I don't know if getting someone to threaten Bruno and Bennie is right. That could blow up in our faces. Bruno and Bennie might try to cut a deal with the DA if they think we don't have their backs. But we still need to do something."

Edwards said, "Well, as of right now, Bruno and Bennie are only being charged with threatening the prof. We could hire a good lawyer who is used to dealing with these kinds of cases. Maybe get the lawyer to meet with Bruno and Bennie. Have the lawyer try to get them out on bail. We pick up the tab."

Welborn yelled, "But we're already in a financial hole. We've got a number of clients who are very pissed about how their bets have been paying out of late. Do we have the money to hire a fancy lawyer for Bruno and Bennie?"

Forman said, "I don't think we have much choice. Bruno and Bennie could surely get some deal with the DA if they want to cooperate. We need to get them on our side and for them to stay there."

"Then we need to find a lawyer, have the lawyer talk to Bruno and Bennie, and make sure that Bruno and Bennie will be taken care of financially," said Edwards.

Welborn yelled again, "You want to spend more money on Bruno and Bennie even when I told you we'd had a bad run lately on our bets and customers? That's crazy!"

Forman said, "As I said, we don't have much choice. Bruno and Bennie could roast us if they wanted to. We must keep them on our side; money is the best way. Bruno and Bennie are not big players, so if we offer them ten grand each, that's a lot of money for those two. They will be very grateful for our gesture because ten grand is important to them. It will at least buy us some time."

Edwards suggested, "Okay, I know a lawyer downtown who would help us out. He's been involved in some cases that included money laundering and extortion. The guy likes to think he's above that kind of work but does whatever it takes when his business gets tight. I can put a call into him and get it set up. He will need a retainer, so we must factor that in on what this will cost."

"Hell, as much as this sounds like it will cost," said Welborn, "We might as well cash out now and head to the islands like we were going to do at the end of the season."

Forman smiled and said, "You know we can't do that. We've got a lot of money on the streets, and we also owe a good amount. If we hightail it out of town, you know someone would come looking for us, and they won't be there to say hi. Most of our customers are just regular gamblers, but you both know we have some who have ties to the mob. Just trying to hit the road is pretty risky. Plus, we've spent a lot of time and money developing our businesses. When we talked about hitting the road after the season, I assumed we would eventually return to Philly. I don't have a fallback plan for my long-term career aspirations. I figured things would settle down while we were away, but we could still return. You guys didn't think that?"

Welborn and Edwards both nodded in unison. Edwards said, "Yeah, you're right. I also thought our trip to the islands would be temporary. We know a lot about the gambling business in Philly, and I don't want to start over in another city."

Welborn said, "I guess I also agree. But we really have to have things straightened out with Bruno and Bennie. Can't have any loose ends."

"Loose ends?" said Forman. "Are you suggesting that we might have to have Bruno and Bennie taken care of?"

"I'm not that we need to do that right now, but if things blow up with the DA and the cops, we may have to take drastic action. That's just the way things might go."

Both Forman and Edwards exchanged glances. Neither of them seemed as ready as Welborn was on having Bruno and Bennie killed if need be, but they both knew that Welborn would indeed play that card if necessary. They both nodded to Welborn.

Things seemed to be getting more complicated with every turn for the gamblers. But they, indeed, weren't ready for what was coming next!

Chapter Twenty-Five

Ineeded to set up a meeting with Maury Johnson, the accounting manager for the Linc's vendors. I discovered he was in charge of all the different vendor accounts. He was responsible for gathering all the info and then comparing all the results to see how each of the vendors performed. Then he was responsible for ensuring each vendor received its share of the sales after Aramark took their fee.

I tried very hard to get in contact with Johnson. I called but never heard back. I found his email address but got no response either. I didn't want to jump to conclusions, but the fact that he was dodging me didn't make me feel confident about whatever he might later say.

Finally, I just decided to take a trip down to the Linc. I went to the office and asked the receptionist for Johnson's office. She told me where his office was on the third floor. I went straight to the third floor and found his office. The door was open, and a man was sitting at the desk. I said, "Sorry to bother you, but are you, Maury Johnson?"

The man at the desk said, "I am, but I don't remember having an appointment with anyone at this time."

"You don't have one. My name is Dr. Ben Stone. I'm a professor at Temple, but I am working for Aramark to look into your accounts payable down here at the Linc."

Johnson's face immediately had a scowl on it. He said, "I have been receiving your calls and emails, but I've been swamped. Sorry, I didn't get back to you. We are coming up on tax season, and I've got a lot of information I need to figure out. I've got a boatload of financial statements to produce and get started on all the tax returns that will be due soon. I've got a lot of partnership returns as well as limited liability returns. They're not due right now, but I need to get a jump on them. Anyway, have a seat. What are you specifically looking at?"

I sat down and replied, "Aramark gave me access to all your vendor accounts, and I've been examining if there are any irregularities. I'm sorry to say that I have found some."

Johnson was clearly taken aback, but he put on a brave face. "What types of irregularities?"

"I ran some statistical analyses, and it looks like some of your accounts have receipts that aren't making their way into Aramark's receivable accounts. Simply put, it looks like a substantial amount of money is not properly accounted for." I decided to throw the guy a bone for now. "I'm sure there is a valid reason, but I just needed your help figuring it out. Obviously, you certainly know much more about the accounts than I do." Okay, now I was pandering to Johnson.

My bone toss didn't have much of an effect. Johnson's face now had an even more edgy look. He was clearly caught off guard. But what was most telling was that I could tell he was trying to figure out a reasonable explanation for any discrepancies quickly. He said, "I'm sure I can figure out what has happened. As I said, tax season is upon me, and I have a lot of things going on. I always have a number of vendor accounts that are difficult to reconcile at year-end, so it's not surprising that some things need to be adjusted. Are there particular accounts that concern you?"

I said, "A few specific ones stand out, but there seems to be an overall pattern. You probably know about Benford's Law. I used it for the totality of the Linc's vendors, and there seems to be a consistent shortage of monies across a large number of accounts. Any idea why that might be the case?"

Johnson squirmed in his chair and replied, "Well, like I said, a number of adjustments need to be done for the year-end audit. Happens every year."

"I understand that, but I'm not talking about financial statements or tax returns. I'm looking at cash flow statements, and there appears to be some money missing."

"Well, Dr. Stone, as I said, things are hectic, so I'm sure I can't answer your questions right now. Why don't you list the specific accounts you find concerning, and I will get back to you as soon as possible?"

That was the answer I was expecting. A little obfuscation and a lot of delays. It sounds like what we see on TV about politicians trying to avoid the questions. I said, "I have a spreadsheet that lays out the accounts in question. I was hoping you could look at them and provide a reasonable explanation. And I know you are busy, but I would be grateful if you could get back to me with some answers in a few days. Do you think you can do that?"

Johnson replied, "Of course. Give me a couple of days, and I'll be in touch. And I'm sorry you have so many questions that need to be answered, but I'm sure I can provide you with the answers you need."

Johnson stood up and extended his hand. I took it and said, "Just make sure you get back to me with some answers in a few days. I'm also under a bit of pressure."

Johnson nodded and smiled. As I left his office, I was sure of two things. One: Johnson was involved in siphoning off a good deal of cash from the Linc accounts, and two: I was never going to hear from Maury Johnson ever again.

I was going to have to get Aramark involved right now. If my take on Johnson was even partially correct, Maury was going to disappear very quickly, and he would be taking a ton of cash with him. In fact, I may have to get Sharon to help me. For a non-CPA, Sharon was exceptionally talented at figuring out how to handle many aspects of financial fraud.

And that's precisely what was going on down at the Linc!

Chapter Twenty-Six

Since Sharon and I both had several questions we needed to discuss with the management down at the Linc, she called and got us an appointment with the football manager of the Eagles: Bill James. Franklin Johns had already made a call, too. James called Sharon, and she told him some of the questions she had, and James said that he would make sure that the head football coach, John Starr, would also be available

We decided to drive down to the Linc. We thought about just taking the subway or Uber, but since we would be doing some "official" business, we opted to be a little more professional in our approach. Sharon dressed a little, and I wore my blue suit and red power tie. We knew we would meet a football coach and a manager who would both likely be in jeans and sweats, but clothes make the man and woman.

We found a spot for guest parking. We headed to the office, and a guy who appeared to be the admin person told us to have a seat. He knew we were there to talk to James and Starr and said that both would be out very soon.

After about fifteen minutes, a tall, muscular man greeted us. He said, "I'm Bill James, the manager of the Eagles," as he stuck out his hand to both of us.

Sharon took his hand first and said, "I'm Detective Sharon Levin. Please call me Sharon." Then I extended my hand and said, "Dr. Ben Stone. Nice to meet you."

"Nice to meet both of you," replied James. "Coach Starr will meet us at my office. He's finishing up some of his plans for this week's game."

We went down a hallway into an office. The office was covered in football memorabilia. There were plaques, pictures, and trophies everywhere. James pointed to two chairs. "Have a seat."

We sat, and James said, "So we'll wait for Coach Starr before we begin in earnest, but I'm sure this has to do with Franklin Johns and maybe Billy Sans. However, honestly, I don't know why Dr. Stone is here. I can speak for both of us when I say that Coach Starr and I know absolutely nothing about accounting."

I smiled and said, "Please call me Ben, and I don't know much about football, but there seems to be a possible link between football and accounting down at the Linc. I probably won't have much to say, but Sharon thought I might be able to help shed some light on what might be going down at the Linc."

At that moment, a very tall and well-developed man entered the door. He held his hand to me and said, "I'm Coach Starr, but call me John."

"My name is Ben, and this is Detective Levin. An honor to meet you."

"I'm not sure it's an honor," he said. "It might be an honor if we can make a long run into the playoffs."

All four of us laughed, and Sharon said, "Please call me Sharon, and while I will admit that I'm not a huge football fan, I was born and raised here in Philly, so I know that the Eagles are important. I hope your team can finish the season with some wins and make a long run into the playoffs."

Starr smiled and said, "That's the plan. Anyway, what can Bill and I do for you?"

Sharon replied, "Well, as you know, the police have been looking into the death of Len Meadows of the Giants. We've made some headway, but I wanted to discuss how Franklin Johns is progressing with rehab. It appears that Johns and his rehab are more than just about football. We believe Meadows's death relates to Johns and his ACL injury. I know you have provided Johns with security, and I wanted to know if you think that has been working?"

James replied, "I think it has been working well. Franklin has round-the-clock protection. He is driven to rehab and is never without someone to cover him. To be honest, I think he's getting tired of it, but he doesn't want to take any chances. Simply put, he hasn't tried to sneak away. And I would bust his ass if he tried to."

Sharon said, "You have a good security plan right now. I'm not asking because I want to bet on a game, but do you have a prognosis on whether he will return before the season ends?"

Starr replied, "Chances are about seventy-five percent, maybe higher. I will tell you that we are developing a game plan that includes Franklin in the mix."

"That sounds good. I also wanted to discuss Billy Sans, the replacement for Franklin. I know you are providing any additional security for Sans. Everything going okay there?"

"Same as Franklin. Round-the-clock security" said, James. "Should we be more worried?"

"I don't know for sure, but I can say that I have been around a lot of gambling and betting. Gamblers will do many ugly things to make their bets work out. I don't have the relationship nailed down between the gamblers and the guys who threatened Ben, but I've got a feeling they are related. And Ben thinks these gamblers might be related to the missing money he is tracking down at the Linc."

James said, "I didn't know money was unaccounted for at the Linc. What's going on?"

I said, "My investigation is about how some accounting of accounts payable down at the Linc doesn't reconcile. Aramark hired me to look at their books. I'm sure a lot of money is being pilfered through the accounting systems at the Linc. I can't prove that the gamblers Sharon is chasing are in cahoots with the accounts payable issue, but they are starting to look pretty connected."

Sharon added, "As Ben said, we don't have anything nailed down between Franklin, Len Meadows, and the accounting irregularities, but we're getting closer. But I know from experience that gamblers, particularly ones in a hole, will do whatever it takes. If that means finding a way for Billy Sans to go down with an injury before Franklin returns, they'll do it in a minute. By the way, who would be next in line if Sans goes down?"

Coach Starr replied, "A rookie. He's progressing well in his development, but he is way behind Franklin and Billy."

Sharon said, "So keeping Sans healthy would be a good idea wouldn't it be?"

Starr replied, "I'll ensure that Billy's security is iron tight. We can't take a chance. And I appreciate your taking the time to bring us up to speed on what seems to be happening."

"Just doing our jobs," Sharon said.

James said, "Well, even though you both don't seem to be big football fans, I'm going to get you two some great tickets. In fact, I will even let you bring as many people as you want."

Sharon and I looked at each other and smiled. She said, "Thank you so much for the offer. How about we wait until we clear up some of this stuff between Franklin, Meadows, gambling, and the Linc? I know that I would enjoy the game much more if we've brought some of these scumbags to justice."

Starr smiled and inquired, "Did you play any sports growing up?"

"I was pretty good at softball. Why do you ask?"

"Because you have that kickass attitude that successful athletes thrive on."

Sharon smiled and said, "I'm not sure I'm kickass, but I take my job very seriously. So does Ben, but he usually doesn't have to hold anyone at gunpoint as I sometimes do."

James said, "Staring down at a huge bunch of accounting numbers can sometimes be pretty scary, too. Just in a different way."

As I stood there, I thought, for a football manager, this guy understood the way of the world. Much more than just football.

But none of us knew how quickly things would happen.

Chapter Twenty-Seven

Welborn got a call on his cell phone very early on Friday morning. He answered the call and said, "Who the fuck is this? It's too early to be calling me."

"It's Maury Johnson down at the Linc. We've got a problem."

Welborn already felt he had too many problems, so he didn't need more. He said, "Great. I've already got a bunch of shit going on right now. What problem do you have?"

"We've got an accounting professor looking into the books down at the Linc. I met with him yesterday, and I think this guy has already figured out what we've been doing. He may be just an egghead professor, but he seems to know what he's doing."

Welborn cursed and said, "This fucking professor is becoming a major pain in my ass. So is his girlfriend, the cop. I'm trying to put some money together; all that seems to happen these days is spending more and more and making less and less. Did you get a plan to handle this, professor? How much do we have squirreled away right now?"

Johnson replied, "I've got about $600K that we can split down the middle."

"Only 300 large for us? I thought we would have a lot more than that."

"I've tried to be careful about how much we've filtered into our pockets. The Linc's accountants are very thorough, so I had to be careful."

Welborn said, "Apparently not careful enough since this professor must have figured out what we've been doing. Anyway, what's your plan?"

"About all I can think of to do is hit the road. I think this prof has enough info to get me into trouble with the cops or maybe even the FBI. Time to put some miles between Philly and me right now."

"So, I assume you will get our share to us?"

"Of course. I need to pull a lot of cash out of our accounts down at the Linc and other places, and then I'll get you your share."

Welborn said, "How do I know you're getting us a fair cut?"

Johnson said, "You're getting a fair share because I know you and your partners know some muscle guys, and you could come after me. I'm not stupid enough to try to cheat you. I can't give you a breakdown of the money right now, but I can soon. But I think it's more important right now to gather the 300K in cash for you as soon as possible. It probably will take me about two or three days. Is that okay?"

Welborn pondered momentarily and then said, "Alright, I will trust you for now. But remember that we know some guys who can track you down if we find out you stiffed on any of the dough."

"As I said, I'm not dumb enough to try to screw you. We've been making decent money for a few years now, and I know you guys would not take kindly to being screwed. I'm going to make sure that you get your share in total. Don't worry. I'll be in touch once I get the money pulled together and am ready to get your share to you."

Welborn said, "I guess that's about all we can do right now. Just remember to make sure we get our dough. We've already had to bring in some muscle, so doing it again is not a problem."

"I know better than to try to stiff you guys. I'll be in touch as soon as I have the cash." Johnson then hung up the phone.

Welborn decided to make an instant cup of coffee. After pouring his coffee, he sat for a few minutes and thought. He wasn't happy with how things had been going of late. He's got the lady cop on his ass, the accounting prof is digging into the Linc, and he was trusting Bruno and Bennie not to give up info about the murder of the football player. He had a lot of things bouncing around in his head right now. If all of this were going to work out, he would have to talk to his partners and make big decisions quickly.

It was 7 a.m., a bit early for gamblers. Welborn didn't care, and he called Forman first and then Edwards. He got them out of bed and told them they needed to get into the office. They both complained about the hour, but Welborn was emphatic that they needed to come in. Both growled but agreed.

Forman got to the office first in about a half-hour. He was drinking an extra-large Dunkin Donuts coffee. Welborn told Forman to wait for Edwards before they talked. He told Forman to enjoy his coffee.

About 15 minutes later, Edwards came in with a Venti Starbucks in his hand. Everyone needed their caffeine jolt.

Edwards was the first to speak. "What's the emergency? We've got a plan, and we should stick to it."

Welborn said, "Plan is going to have to change. Maury, the accounting guy down at the Linc, thinks that the accounting professor is on to our scheme with the accounts payable money."

Forman thundered, "Shit! What are we going to do now? Also, how much money does Maury available right now?"

"Maury says that our share of the Linc scam is about $300,000," replied Welborn.

Edwards jumped in and said, "Bullshit. It's got to be more than that. Maury is just lying to us."

"Maybe, but I don't think so. Maury has been pretty solid for us for several years. Maybe he skates a little off the top, but Maury knows that if we catch him screwing us too much, we'll have somebody go talk to him."

Forman said, "Yeah, bringing muscle has worked great so far. Bruno and Bennie are still in jail; now Maury's a problem. And Franklin Johns may be back on the field before the season ends. Yeah, things are going just great."

"That's why we need to move up our time frame," said Welborn. "We can't wait for the Eagles versus Giants game and see if Johns is available. We're going to have to take a gamble on a game this weekend. A big gamble because we need the dough."

Edwards said, "So you think we should just be gamblers like all the suckers we've seen over the years who have lost everything.

Shit, we don't gamble. We make informed decisions and don't just bet."

"I know," said Welborn. "But right now, we'll have to go on a limb. Many things are going against us, and we need to make a move. Anyone got a game this weekend that we should bet heavily on?"

Neither Forman nor Edwards jumped to answer. All three gamblers just sat for a moment. Finally, Edwards said, "Cowboys over the Eagles. Eagles are two-point favorites with Billy Sans still in at running back."

Forman said, "But Sans had a good game his last time out. Two points aren't much of a margin for error."

Edwards replied, "That's true, but Sans usually isn't that good. The Cowboys aren't great, but they're doing well over the last few games. We can just roll the dice and bet heavily on the Cowboys covering the spread."

Both Welborn and Forman didn't say anything immediately, but finally, Welborn said, "I don't like to gamble, but I don't think we have much choice right now. We'll bet all we have on the Cowboys to cover."

It was a risky play, but all three gamblers felt they had no choice: The Cowboys to cover on Sunday. And since all three were Catholic, they crossed themselves.

Chapter Twenty-Eight

It's Sunday. The Eagles are playing the Cowboys at the Linc. The game is at 1 p.m., so tailgating starts at 8:00 a.m. The grills were fired up. The beer was flowing. Everyone wore their Eagles hats, shirts, and all the other gameday paraphernalia. The team was having a good season. The Cowboys started the season slowly but have been on a run for the last month. It was likely to be a good game.

The Eagles won the toss and elected to defer until the second half. Thus, the Cowboys had the first possession. The first half was pretty dull. Neither team had much of a chance to score. In the second quarter, the Eagles scored a field goal and thus were up 3-0. That's the way the first half ended. The defensive units of both teams had strong first halves.

The Eagles got the ball to start the second half. Again, both teams were quite strong defensively at the beginning of the half. Finally, with about three minutes to go in the third quarter, the Cowboys ran a trick play by setting up an end-around, but then the receiver passed the ball back to the quarterback. He found an open wide receiver, and the Cowboys scored a touchdown. The extra point was good, and the Cowboys were up 7-3. The gamblers were hoping the game ended that way.

Billy Sans did not have an excellent game. He had run the ball 12 times for only thirty yards. He hadn't come close to scoring. The Eagles began a drive at their 30-yard line with only three minutes left on the game clock. The offensive coordinator decided to start with some running plays. Billy had a 12-yard run on the next play. The Eagles ran again, and Billy gained 15 yards. The offensive coordinator decided to stick with the run, and Billy ran for another 10 yards. The two-minute warning was given. While the coaches huddled with the quarterback, Billy came to the coach and told him that he saw openings on the left side on each play. The coach decided to stay on the ground unless it became necessary to throw the ball.

Billy ran up the left side on the next play and gained another twelve yards. The Eagles were now at the 21-yard line with a minute and a half to go. The Eagles stayed on the ground. Billy ran twice, and they were at the 10-yard line with a minute to play. The next play was a pass that fell incomplete. Then the quarterback called an audible for Billy, and he ran straight up the middle for a touchdown. The extra point was good, and the Eagles were up 10-7 with thirty-38 seconds left.

The Cowboys tried a couple of 20-yard passes and completed one of them. They were at midfield. They tried one bomb to the endzone that was blocked by a defensive back. The Cowboys tried a lateral back trick play with only 10 seconds left. They made some progress and reached the 20-yard line when the Cowboy wide receiver was tackled as time expired.

The Eagles fans erupted in cheers. The gamblers did not.

The gamblers don't usually watch that many games but had decided to watch this one since they had a lot riding on it. Welborn said, "How the fuck did Sans have such an incredible number of runs during that final few minutes? The guy did nothing for most of the game. Then he decides to be Franklin Johns for two minutes, and we lose. That sucks."

Forman said, "How the Eagles won doesn't matter. What matters is that they did, and we are screwed. We bet a ton on this game for the Cowboys to cover. One point made the difference between us being flush and broke. We've got a real problem. Actually, a couple of them."

Edwards said, "Well, we said we were going to hit the road even if we won. Now we have a moral imperative to leave. We had some bets out this week to some guys who are wired into the local mob. They are not going to take kindly to us stiffing them on their bets."

"Yeah, but if we skip out on all our debts, we can't return to Philly," said Forman.

"You got a better idea?" said Welborn. "We need to put together as much cash as we can. Maury has already said we should net about 300K for the Linc scam, plus what we have on hand."

Edwards said, "That's not going to be a lot of money. Plus, we still have the issue of Bernie and Bennie. The lawyer I talked to said he needs ten large as a retainer, and Bernie and Bennie need 50 large for bail."

"Nothing we can do about that," said Forman. "We've all got about $200,000 each available, plus what Maury brings in. It's not a huge sum, but it's what we have. Bernie and Bennie are on their own."

"But they can tell a few tales about us," said Edwards.

"If they cut a deal, the only thing they will give up is that we were behind getting them to threaten the professor," said Welborn. "They're not going to give up the football player Meadows. They killed the guy, which is a capital offense for them. They'll keep their mouths shut about that."

Forman said, "You sure? Bernie and Bennie are not the sharpest tools in the shed. They might tell the cops everything."

"They're pretty stupid, but not that stupid," replied Welborn. "Anyway, all we can do is gather what cash we can and find an island that doesn't have extradition laws with the U.S. We let things cool down for a few months, then set up shop in another city. Sorry fellas, but Philly is now closed to us."

Forman and Edwards nodded in agreement. They didn't know that I have a good friend, Mikayla Heston, at FinCEN, whose job is to track large cash transactions. And Maury Johnson would be doing just that with the cash from the Linc!

Chapter Twenty-Nine

Maury knew he was going to have a challenging day. He had a lot of things to get straight and get straight in a hurry. He had almost all the money he had stolen from the Linc set up in various regular bank accounts. He had always just spread the money around. At first, he thought he could move his share of the money to Switzerland or the Caymans, but he had never before used those means to move money. And he didn't have time to find someone who could help him. Plus, he had to get the gamblers their share, which had to be in cash.

He had continually siphoned off a little at a time, moved it to cash, and then given their share to the gamblers. He had never moved that much dough. He had also kept his cash transactions below the $10,000 threshold to keep the Feds and others from thinking anything was amiss. But he didn't have time to do that now, so he just started pulling the maximum amount he could withdraw from all the bank accounts he had set up. Fortunately, he had over 30 different bank accounts from which he could withdraw funds. The problem for Maury was that he didn't know about FinCEN!

As Maury was furiously pulling funds from wherever he could, Mikayla Heston was having a regular day at FinCEN. Well, it was until she got an alert about unusual withdrawals in the Philadelphia area. She started to pull information about withdrawals from several bank accounts, all just under the $10,000 threshold. It was a huge red flag for her.

She tracked down some of the accounts and discovered many were in the same physical vicinity as Philly. There were a lot of banks, but that didn't concern Mikayla. She logged into a database FinCEN uses to see where money is moving and how quickly the money could be removed. Clearly, someone was cleaning out a lot of money from many accounts and making the rounds to several banks to pick up the cash.

Mikayla at first thought about contacting the local FBI office, but then she thought of another way: She could call me. Mikayla, Sharon, and I had become close friends, so she had my cell phone number.

She called me, and I picked up on the second ring. "Hello," I said.

"Ben, it's Mikayla Heston at FinCEN. How are you doing?"

"Great to hear from you. I'm doing well. I've got a class in about two hours and just reading an academic article. What's going on?"

Mikayla replied, "I just got an alert that someone is moving a lot of cash in your area. I called you before I went to the FBI because the FBI has a lot of procedures I need to go through before they can take action, and whoever is moving this dough is in a big hurry. If I had to guess, I think whoever it is is planning on getting out of town. If I give you an address, any chance Sharon might be able to arrest whoever is doing this before they make a run for it?"

I replied, "Have you already tracked down an address?"

"Most transactions are in Northeast Philly, but surprisingly, some are down at the Linc. There are few, but just a few, which is a little weird."

I thought briefly and said, "Not surprising at all, Mikayla. I've been working for Aramark as a consultant and examining the books for the vendors at the Linc. I recently found out about money that was missing from Linc's accounts. In fact, I just confronted the accounting manager yesterday. I thought I was on to something, but it must be bigger than I thought if the guy is already cashing out."

"What's his name?"

"Maury Johnson."

Mikayla ran through one of her databases, looking for any names associated with any accounts she had flagged. She told me, "There are a lot of names on these accounts, but Maury got a little sloppy. His name pops up the most by far. That's the guy."

"Give me all the addresses you have. I will call Sharon and see if she can get a judge she knows to issue an arrest warrant. She often has one judge she works with who will issue a warrant over the phone. Let me call her, and I'll get back to you."

"Thanks so much. Let me know what's going on when you can."

I called Sharon at her office. She picked up and said, "Are you calling me this early to discuss dinner?"

"No. I'm calling because Mikayla Heston at FinCEN thinks the guy I told you about regarding the money at the Linc is cashing out. She has the guy's addresses, home, and office, and she's hoping you can convince a friendly judge to issue an arrest warrant. Any chance you could pull that off?"

"Give me the particulars. I'll get to work on it right now."

Meanwhile, Bernie and Bennie were getting some terrible news. They figured the gamblers would get an attorney and get them out of jail. All the cops had on Bernie, and Bennie was threatening the professor. Bernie and Bennie thought they needed to sit tight and everything would work out.

Bernie was sitting in his cell when one of the guards came to him and told him he had a phone call. Bernie went to the pay phone and took the call. "Who is this?" he asked.

"This is Melvin Swartz. I'm an attorney who was supposed to get you and Bennie Wilson out on bail."

"Why aren't we out? It's been four days since we've been in jail. How long does it take to post bail?"

"The problem is that I called the guys who were to fund your bail, and one of them told me that he doesn't have the money to post your bail."

Bernie yelled, "Are you fucking kidding me? We need to get cut loose, and we need to have it happen now."

"Sorry, but there is nothing I can do. I'll contact you if I get my retainer amount and the money for bail." He hung up.

Bernie slammed the phone down. The guard took him back to his cell, which was right next to Bennie's. Bernie told Bennie through the wall, "The bastards who were supposed to get us out on bail aren't coming through. Assholes are leaving us to hang in the breeze."

Bennie said, "Then we don't owe those guys anything. Tell one of the guards that we must talk to a cop or a lawyer about what happened with the professor. We'll cut a deal with the DA by giving information about Welborn, Forman, and Edwards. It's time to take care of ourselves."

Bernie replied, "Yep, fuck those guys. We are on our own."

Chapter Thirty

Sharon called in a favor with a friendly judge to get a warrant for Johnson's house in Ardmore. She took two uniforms with her over to Johnson's home.

Once they got to the home, Sharon knocked on his door and said, "This is the police. You need to open the door."

Sharon and the uniforms were heard shuffling around in the back of the house. One of the uniforms ran around to the back door. Just as he arrived, he saw Johnson trying to scurry out the back. The cop took his gun out and said, "Just stop there. You're not going anywhere."

Sharon and the other cop came around back. Both cops smiled at her, and one said, "You can have the pleasure."

Sharon smiled back and took out her cuffs. She said, "Put your hands behind your back, Mr. Johnson. I'm going to give you your Miranda rights. Then, we'll get you into that patrol car and head downtown."

Johnson didn't say anything other than he wanted a lawyer. The standard response to getting arrested.

On their way downtown, Sharon called me to tell me Johnson was in custody. She said the guy had already asked for a lawyer, but we'll see if he had anything to say. She said she'd be in touch.

I called Mikayla, and she picked up the phone as soon as it rang. "FinCEN, Mikayla Heston."

"Mikayla, it's Ben Stone. Sharon got him!"

"Are you kidding? That's amazing. I thought that guy was already in the wind."

"He was probably almost out the door when Sharon got to his house in Ardmore. Sharon said she quickly looked around and saw bundles of cash all over the house. She's just guessing, but she thought at least $200,000 looked ready to move. She thinks she got there maybe an hour or so before Johnson would be gone."

Mikayla said, "Wow, we were so lucky that Sharon knows a judge. No way the FBI would have made it in time."

"Sometimes it's not what you know, but who. And yes, we lucked out on the timing. Actually, I feel a little stupid that I didn't consider Johnson might run off once I confronted him about the money with the Linc. I should have given Sharon the heads-up to be on the lookout for Johnson to make a move."

"Ben, you've got a lot on your table. Plus, there's no way for even Sharon to get a warrant without the info I provided. I doubt any judge would have issued a warrant with what you had. Maybe, but I doubt it. Plus, Ben, we did this whole thing by the book. That's key when it's time to go before a judge. If Johnson has any sense, he will be looking for some sort of deal. I don't know what he has he can use, but if he's been in this business for any time, I'm sure he's got something he can leverage into getting a reduced sentence."

"Wow, it's clear that you have a lot of experience with this type of financial fraud."

Mikayla said, "It's what I do, Ben. Anyway, keep me apprised of what's going on. And please tell Sharon that I appreciate her assistance."

"I'll be in touch." With that, I hung up.

Meanwhile, Bernie and Bennie tried to convince an assistant DA that they knew a lot of important information they would give the assistant DA if he dropped the charges for threatening me. At first, the assistant DA wasn't that interested, but then Bernie convinced him that all the info about illegal gambling was worth enough that Bennie and he should get a walk. Bernie told him about unlawful gambling in Philly to whet the assistant DA's appetite. Finally, the assistant DA decided that Bernie and Bennie probably had enough to offer and agreed that he would drop their charges.

Bernie told the assistant DA about Welborn, Forman, and Edwards' gambling operation. He told him about all the money that moved through their doors and that they had been at this for years. He told the assistant DA where their office was.

The assistant DA returned to the same judge Sharon used and got a warrant for Welborn, Forman, and Edwards. Three uniformed cops showed up at the gamblers' office. All three were there, and the cops saw huge stacks of cash lying around the office. The cops took the gamblers into custody and read them their rights. Just like Johnson, the first thing they said was they wanted a lawyer.

It was then that things got interesting!

Johnson wanted to speak to another assistant DA. He met with Johnson, and Johnson said that he could provide information about his accomplices with the scams at the Linc. He wanted a deal to walk free and clear, and he would give out the names. The DA initially thought that wasn't enough, but after thinking about it, he offered Johnson a reduced sentence, but not a walk. Johnson decided to take the deal and gave up Welborn, Forman, and Edwards.

Once the assistant DA heard the names, he knew they were the same ones involved with Bernie and Bennie. He made some calls and found that the gamblers were already in custody based on Bernie and Bennie's information. He called the DA and told him many things were coming together with all these cases.

Welborn, Forman, and Edwards were in custody in the Northeast. They were separated, and the investigators tried to play some Prisoners' Dilemma with the three being played against each other. At first, the three could hold their own, but as the pressure built, Forman decided to cave. He told the investigators about the Linc scam, but the investigators said it wasn't enough. In a state of panic, Forman turned on Bernie and Bennie and confessed to the murder of Meadows, and for that, Forman was given a reduced sentence on all his charges.

By the end of the day, Johnson eventually got a walk. Forman got a reduced sentence for gambling and paying for Bernie and Bennie to attack Meadows. Welborn and Edwards got rung up for a whole load of gambling and the conspiracy with the Meadows event. The real losers, and they should have been, were Bernie and Bennie, who were charged with the murder of Len Meadows!

All in all, it was a day when justice was the winner!

Chapter Thirty-One

After the news of what happened in these cases broke, Sharon and I had a bit of a celebrity for a few days. I think it added to the interest since NFL football players were involved. Before it started to wind down, even Dr. Bagley and Mikayla from FinCEN made the news, not that either wanted to be there. Dr. Bagley was quite pleased that his job was back to normal. Mikayla just went back to her position looking for the financial fraud case. Even the news that Franklin Johns would be playing in the Giants game at the end of the season added to the good news. But Bagley, Mikayla, Linda, Sharon, and I all got one more surprise.

It was the Thursday before the Eagles game up at MetLife Stadium. It was late afternoon, and Sharon had come home early. I was grading some exams, and Sharon was watching TV. There was a knock at my door.

With how things have been going regarding people coming to our house, Sharon carefully opened the peephole. She recognized Franklin Johns in an instant.

She opened the door and said, "Franklin. It's great to see you. I heard you are playing this weekend. Great news. However, what brings you by? In fact, how did you find us?"

Franklin replied, "Good to see you, too. I found out where you live by asking my security detail. One of the guys knew your address from one of your previous cases. I wanted to see you in person. By the way, please introduce me to your friend."

I came over to the door, and Sharon said to Franklin, "This is my better half, Dr. Ben Stone. He was involved in this whole craziness, too."

Franklin and I shook hands. Franklin's hand was immense, and his hand dwarfed mine. He said, "Nice to meet you, Dr. Stone."

"Please call me Ben. Do you want to come in?"

"Actually, I can't. We have a game film to watch in about an hour, so I must return to the stadium. But there is something I want to give you." He handed me five tickets. "These are five tickets for the tenth row at the game this Sunday. I have one each for you two, one for Dr. Bagley, who did my surgery, and one for the woman I heard helped a lot in this whole thing. Mikayla, I think I heard. And finally, one for the woman who helped track the fraud down at the Linc."

I said, "Wow, that is very generous, but all of us were doing our jobs. Even my involvement was with a consulting case, so I got paid, too."

Franklin said, "Yeah, but all of you five were instrumental in my getting back on the field and being safe while all the nuttiness was going on. I just wanted to say thank you."

Sharon said, "As Ben said, that is very generous, and unlike Ben, I'll accept them without hesitation. I haven't been to an Eagles game in years."

Franklin said, "Since you haven't been to one in a while, I hope we have a good game. I'm probably not going to get to play that much. The rehab team cleared me to play, but the coach didn't want to risk me that much. If we win this game, we will be in the playoffs, and the coach wants to ensure that I am available. But I'll jump in if something happens to Billy. We need this one!"

Sharon said, "We will keep our fingers crossed that we win. And thank you again for the tickets."

"One more thing. The game starts at 4 p.m., so if you are leaving Philly to get to MetLife Stadium, I suggest you leave about 10 a.m."

Sharon said, "We'll try to gather everyone at our house and leave from here. Thanks again."

Franklin left, and I told Sharon, "You get the tickets to Dr. Bagley, and I'll take care of Mikayla and Linda. I don't know if they are available, but I hope so."

"Me, too."

It turned out that Bagley, Mikayla, and Linda were all available and excited about attending the game. We decided to meet Bagley, Mikayla, and Linda at our house early Sunday morning. Then I would take our car, and we could travel together. It would be a little tight, but we would make it work. The game wasn't until 4 p.m.

When Sunday came, everyone met at our house at the appropriate time. We were getting ready to leave when there was a knock at my door. I looked through the peephole again and saw a man wearing a uniform and hat.

I opened the door and asked, "Hi. What can I do for you?"

"My name is Roy Lester. I am the driver for your trip up the game this afternoon. The limo is right around the corner. Courtesy of Franklin Johns."

All five of us just stared at each other for a moment. Finally, Sharon broke the silence and said, "Might as well pile in, folks. It looks like we are traveling in style."

We got up to the game at about 1 p.m. We didn't do much tailgating but still had a great time. Bagley wanted to hear about all the adventures Sharon, and I had had. He thought the vampires down in New Orleans were fascinating.

The game was quite exciting. Both teams played well. Billy Sans had an excellent game which was fortunate because the quarterback for the Giants was passing very well.

The game entered the fourth quarter with the Giants up by four points, 27-23. Only five minutes left when the Eagles got the ball at their 25-yard line. On the first play, Billy ran up the middle. He was tackled on the thirty, but Billy twisted his ankle slightly. He could hobble off the field, but Franklin went into the game.

The first time Franklin ran the ball, he was tackled at the line of scrimmage. It was third down and five. The Eagles quarterback dropped back to pass, but the Giants' rush was coming. The quarterback saw Franklin out of the side of his eye and tossed the ball to him. Franklin caught the ball at the line of scrimmage, faked to the left, and then cut back. He found an opening and started to sprint. The defense tried to close him, but Franklin picked up more speed. He continued to rush toward the endzone. He saw a defensive back coming hard, and Franklin faked like he was running out of bounds to stop the clock. The defensive back slowed a bit, and Franklin then cut to the inside and got around the defensive back. Franklin could see the end zone at the Giant 20-yard line. He accelerated even more and then almost coasted into the end zone. All the Eagles players crowded around Franklin to congratulate him.

The Giants had only two minutes left in the game. Their quarterback tried a couple of passes toward the sidelines, but the Eagles' defense stopped them. With only seconds left on the game clock, the Giants threw a Hail Mary toward the Eagles' end zone. One of the Giants' wide receivers got his hands on the ball, but he couldn't hold on.

The Eagles won!

Our small five-person team cheered a lot even though Giants fans surrounded us. Before the Eagles left the field, Franklin made eye contact and gave us a thumbs-up. We replied with one from all of us.

When we returned to the limo, we were all still very excited about the game and, of course, the outcome. Sharon said, "Well, Ben and I have never been big football fans, but this was great. We may have to rethink and spend a little more time on football."

Bagley, Mikayla, and Linda said they all felt the same way.

I thought to myself: We had solved a few crimes, put two murderers behind bars, and been chauffeured to an exciting NFL football game. Overall, we had all five had a fine few days!

Thank you for reading.

Please review this book. Reviews
help others find Absolutely Amazing eBooks and
inspire us to keep providing these marvelous tales.
If you would like to be put on our email list
to receive updates on new releases,
contests, and promotions, please go to
AbsolutelyAmazingEbooks.com and sign up.

About the Author

Steve McMillan has been a management professor for over 25 years but recently turned to writing mysteries. Steve worked in public accounting and real estate before entering academia and uses those experiences coupled with his academic life to develop his stories about accounting and murder. While Steve uses his own life experiences in his character and plot development, he wishes he was as cool as Ben Stone.

For sales, editorial information, subsidiary rights information
or a catalog, please write or phone or e-mail
AbsolutelyAmazingEbooks
Manhanset House
Shelter Island Hts., New York 11965-0342, US
Tel: 212-427-7139
www.AbsolutelyAmazingEbooks.com
bricktower@aol.com
www.IngramContent.com

For sales in the UK and Europe please contact our distributor,
Gazelle Book Services
White Cross Mills
Lancaster, LA1 4XS, UK
Tel: (01524) 68765 Fax: (01524) 63232
email: jacky@gazellebooks.co.uk

Printed in the USA
CPSIA information can be obtained
at www.ICGtesting.com
LVHW022007170923
758293LV00009B/158/J